WRITERS OF SECOND-LIFE COMMUNITY

SHORT STORY COMPILATION 2024

Many Special Thanks to:

Selina Green
Book Island Publishing Village
Book Island (238, 117, 37)

Forest Coffee Bar,
Sponsored by Finn Bookmite,
Milk Wood (66, 54, 22)

All of the writers who kindly donated short stories to the collection.

Linden Labs.

This project has no official affiliation with Linden Labs.

An ordinary, non-special thanks to SWoodham,
without whom this book would have been something else.

No AI content has been used in the stories here.
All of the words are 100% hand crafted by humans.
Except possibly for Soen, who is half cat.

No part of this publication may be reproduced or transmitted in any form or by any means, mechanical or electronic including photocopying and recording, or by any information storage and retrieval systems without permission in writing from the author or publisher.

CONTENTS

THE FOUNDATION

by Edmund Broek

[The story takes place around 90 AD in an unnamed coastal city in Ionia (western Asia Minor). It is loosely based on the New Testament "books" 3 John and 2 John. These are very short letters ascribed to John the Evangelist, who is said to have been exiled to the island of Patmos.]

"No further, Gaius," said a rough male voice.

Gaius looked up from the basket he was focusing on, making sure none of the food inside spilled, and found three burly men spread out in a row between him and the door to Diotrephes's house. He recognized them as three ecclesia members - sailors, he thought.

"Ah, hello, Crispus! The peace of the Lord to you!" Gaius cheerfully said and moved to the right to walk around them.

They shifted to block his way. Other worshipers were going straight in, unimpeded. Michael and his family walked right past to the door. Odd, they didn't look at Gaius but had their eyes on the ground. A boy was watching but his mother yanked him along by his arm.

"No further, I said."

"Crispus, what are you talking about? The agape meal is about to begin. I need to get in there."

It was Sunday afternoon, and ecclesia members were gathering for weekly worship to be held in Diotrophes's house, bringing food for themselves and to share. Gaius, like others, was carrying more than was wise and was worried about dropping or spilling things.

"You're not welcome at the agape, Gaius. Go home."

Gaius stood still. He looked into the face of each of the three in turn. Two of them turned away but Crispus held his gaze. Gaius took and released a deep breath. "Crispus, I don't know what's going on, but you can't take it upon yourself to ..."

Crispus interrupted. "We aren't doing this on our own, we're doing what the elders said to do. You have no place here anymore."

"*I'm* an elder. We elders gave no such instructions."

"Look, Gaius, give up. Diotrephes called a meeting, left you out because it was about you, and the elders cut you off. 'Excommunicated' is the fancy word. Which means you ain't welcome at the agape. So go home."

Gaius looked up to the sky in thought or prayer, breathed deeply, then returned his gaze to Crispus. "Ah, well. It's a sad thing. I had hoped and prayed that Diotrephes would come to his senses, but no. I will continue to pray for him and for you also, Crispus, Stephen, and Anicletus. Please pray for me."

He held out the two-handled basket to Crispus. "Now, would you like this food I brought? There's too much for me and anyhow it'll be cold by the time I get it home."

Crispus by reflex reached out to take the woven basket but then instead swept it aside with a blow. It landed askew on the ground. Bread spilled out and a wine jar shattered. Wine seeped out onto and into the earth.

Gaius sighed, then stooped to pick up the basket. The broken pottery clattered as he picked it up. Wine was dripping out the bottom.
"You know, Crispus, you can't hurt me, you can only hurt yourself. Think about it, brother."

He gave a short bow, and walked away, calling out over his shoulder, "Pray for me, brothers."

As Gaius neared his house, a lean teenager bounded from near the door to meet him. "We're almost ready to go to the agape, sir. Why did you come back?"

"Phocas, they cast me out of the ecclesia. Crispus and his friends blocked me from going in."

The youth opened his mouth, then shut it.

Gaius gave him the basket. "Please give this to your mother. Ask her to save what she can. And ask your father to meet me in the courtyard."

Still silent, Phocas set off at a trot around the side of the house towards the back entrance.

Gaius went through the street-side door into the antechamber, then into the small courtyard. He sat down wearily on a wooden bench that faced the rectangular pool in the courtyard's center. Resting his forearms on his thighs he stared at the ground.

Eudokimos, the steward, came out of the kitchen and approached Gaius with slow steps. "What's this that Phocas is chattering about?"

"The elders cast me out of the ecclesia."

Eudokimos wrung his hands and shifted his weight from one foot to the other. "What about us then?"

"I honestly don't know. You should go to the agape if you wish."

"I'll send Phocas to see what he can learn. But what will you do?"

"Today I'll pray here. Tomorrow I'll send a letter to the Elder telling him what they've done. Could you please have someone light the lamps in the gathering room?"

The steward hurried back to the kitchen, calling out to his daughter Niobe and to his son Phocas.

Gaius sat a bit longer, watching the orange-edged clouds in the late afternoon sky over the open courtyard. He heard Niobe go the the ecclesia room and return. Then he stood and went in to pray.

The ecclesia room, as he called it, was a traditional room to the left from the street-side door, re-purposed to new uses. In previous times the men would recline on klinai, gather, drink wine, read poetry, talk politics, argue philosophy, and negotiate deals. But now there were benches and a table. Men, women, and children gathered in it for prayer and agape meals.

Today, however, Gaius was alone. As if sleepwalking he moved to stand in front of the table set apart parallel to the eastern wall. He stood facing the wall, with his back to the tables and benches. He stretched out his arms, palms upward, then placed his hands on the table, closed his eyes, and bowed his head.

A short time later the sounds of voices and sandals broke in on his prayer. He turned, his face showing his confusion. Phocas placed a folded cloth, a small pitcher of wine, a small pitcher of water, bread, and an empty goblet to one side on the wall table. Dorothea, Eudokimos, and Niobe were setting out bread, cheese, olive oil, and roasted fish on one of the free-standing tables. Michael was silhouetted in the doorway. Eudokimos motioned him in, and his family started laying out food on another table.

Eudokimos motioned at what Phocas had brought and said, "Gaius, let's begin."

Gaius said, "Are you certain? There is no easy way back." The adults nodded. Gaius turned back to the table. He took up the bread and broke it, chanting the prayer of thanksgiving.

Gaius, dressed in borrowed laborers' clothing, entered Diotrephes's house through the street door and moved off to the side, still under the portico, not in the courtyard. Everyone, even the servant supposed to be greeting people at the door, had their attention on the discussion inside.

Diotrephes, clad in a plain white tunic, was speaking. He stood on a marble bench in the center of the courtyard. The elders and people were standing around him on all sides to see and hear.

"Despite cautions and exhortations from myself and other elders, Gaius refused to abandon the teachings of John of Patmos and acknowledge the truth of our new teachings. We spoke with him privately and then publicly, as is enjoined by the Gospels and Paul's letters. And we now invite Gaius to repent and return to the ecclesia if he wishes."

"Why wasn't he at the meeting that expelled him?"

"Gaius had no standing to be at the meeting. He had already excommunicated himself from the ecclesia by stubbornly ignoring our brotherly correction. The meeting merely formally recognized the reality."

"But, Diotrephes," spoke up a voice from amidst the listeners, "Gaius was one of the founders here. We know he has helped many of us over the years, and we suspect many more, since he gives in secret."

"The founding was long ago," answered Diotrephes, "and charity is no guarantee of truth. We can remember and even emulate his generosity. But his ties to John of Patmos taint the community and provide an entry point for Satanic teachings."

"Do not forget, Diotrephes," growled a gnarled old man, "that John of Patmos was one of the Twelve. He was there at the Cross and he was the protector and guardian of Mary thereafter. It is no light thing to spurn his teachings and to turn away those whom he sends to us."

"You speak wisely, brother Polychronius. Only manifest errors in core teachings should lead us to resist such a revered person. But as you all know, we have experienced new revelations that John refuses to acknowledge. It is our duty to follow where the Spirit leads and to slough off those who will not accompany us."

Another voice: "No matter what we do, by being in communion with John, Gaius will be in communion with the wider wider ecclesia, Diotrephes."

"John has written that we are 'antichrists.' Gaius, John's disciple, thinks the same. Truly, communion is broken and that is that. Let the wider wider ecclesia wander in the wilderness as it wishes."

Diotrophes sighed, then raised his voice. "The important realities are these: The world is fallen, as we all know. Even followers of the Christ like John are worn down by it, get tired, and lose sight of the truth. To prevent the decay of the Body of Christ in this world, the Spirit must repeatedly intervene to renew the truth, as He has done among us and through us, and as He did through prophet after prophet in Israel. He must prepare pure vessels such as our ecclesia to embody the truth. And we must cast out any impurity."

Gaius's cheeks burned. Out of sight he clenched and unclenched his fists. Then he took a deep breath and eased through the edges of the crowd to go back home.

Shadows flitted as the single oil lamp's flame flickered. All was silent.

Gaius was lost in thought. Witnessing Diotrephes in action had shaken him. "Am I wrong? Are the revelations of Diotrephes and the others true? Is John resisting them only out of pride? Am I?"

He felt as though he was on a makeshift raft on the Aegean Sea, every wave washing over it. You can stare into the depths all you want but you can never tell how deep the water is below you. It might be only chest-deep, or an infinite abyss. And he is nearly alone on his raft. The large established gathering of the Diotrephes ecclesia is a well-crewed boat or even an island, compared with his raft. How Gaius wished John would visit, as his letter promised!

John's letters! In his mind's eye Gaius saw the letters as the dove that brought Noah fresh olive leaves! They prove that beyond the horizon, beyond the empty, churning sea, there is firm land, a continent. He rose, went to the wooden latticework of scrolls, and pulled out John's letters. He brought the lamp and the scrolls to the table and sat down to reread.

John posed a straightforward test of the new revelations: "For many deceivers have gone out into the world who do not confess Jesus the Anointed as coming in the flesh. This is a deceiver and an antichrist."

Earlier he had written, "By this you know the Spirit of God: Every spirit that confesses that Jesus the Anointed has come in the flesh is of God, and every spirit that does not confess that Jesus Christ has come in the flesh is not of God."

Also, "We have seen and testify that the Father has sent the Son as Savior of the world. Whoever confesses that Jesus is the Son of God, God abides in him, and he in God."

Gaius stared upwards from his little sphere of light into the darkness, again lost in thought. "Certainly this a core principle. If Jesus is not God come fully in the flesh but is only God appearing to be a human or working through a human but not actually becoming a human, then He can't redeem humanity and the creation. Hence the principle is not merely abstract words like the philosophers fling about. If Jesus was not truly God and truly human then there is no salvation and Christianity is an empty, cruel fraud. John is right to stand firm on this principle."

The next Lord's Day, twelve people gathered at Gaius's house for the agape meal. Eudokimos, Dorothea, Phocas, and Niobe; Michael, Miriam, and their four children; and the widow Euphrosyne. Word had gone out that the ecclesia at Diotrephes's house had broken communion with Gaius. During the week several people had stopped Gaius in the street to tell him how dismayed they were at this act. Gaius had thanked them and had invited them to his home for the agape. Only the widow and the family, however, had actually walked up the hill to his house on the outskirts of town.

After the prayers and the breaking of the bread and the reception of the bread and wine, they all sat down to eat the food that all had brought.

Miriam was worried. "Once they know we shared the holy meal with you they will cut us off. I'm scared about being cut off from the ecclesia and from the Christ."

Euphrosyne patted her shoulder. "Don't worry, Miriam. It's Diotrephes who should worry. We all know that the ecclesia is Christ's body. He's the head, the ecclesia is the body. The ecclesia everywhere, not just in one town. Each local ecclesia is a member of the body, an organ of the body, as is each of us. "By turning John's people away, and by excommunicating Gaius, the ecclesia of Diotrephes has cut itself off from the wider ecclesia.

She drank from her goblet. "It is as though a finger were to cut itself off the body and declare itself to be the body."

"Ewww!" said one of the boys.

Miriam shushed him. Still frowning, she turned to Michael. He spoke for the first time. "But Diotrephes controls the ecclesia and its teachings. He, and they, can do what they want and no one can stop them."

Euphrosyne said, "Michael, you trade with people from many cities, right?"

"Yes."

"How do you judge which sellers and buyers can be trusted?"

"By my own experience, and by their reputation with people I trust in various cities. A new trader will bring letters of introduction. And word gets around."

"In the same way the ecclesiae in various places learn about other ecclesiae. Some ecclesiae, like Diotrephes's, have embraced false teachings. Over time, other ecclesiae recognize this and break communion with them as people travel back and forth."

"Yes, I see that."

"But the ties among assemblies are much more than trading relationships. The wider ecclesia is Christ's bride. The Holy Spirit guides and protects her, partly through preeminent followers of the Way like John of the Twelve. We are in communion with John and through him with the rest of the wider ecclesia. Diotrephes is not."

Miriam turned away to quell an argument among her kids.

Hearing there were visitors coming, Gaius had not waited for them to be admitted to his house but went out to meet them a short way along the road.

It was a group of five men. Gaius greeted each one in turn, embracing each and exchanging the kiss of peace. One held out a scroll, a letter, but Gaius hurried them to the house, saying first they must wash their feet and recline and eat. There would be time for the letter later.

Gaius looked around. "Now that you have eaten and rested, let me see the letter you brought."

Demetrius said, "The Elder sends his greetings," and passed over a papyrus scroll. Gaius broke the seal, unrolled the scroll, held it closer to a lamp, and began to read quietly but audibly to himself. The others heard individual words, including the name "Diotrephes." They glanced at each other.

Gaius reached the end and looked up and said, "John speaks highly of you, Demetrius." He read aloud: "Testimony has been given on behalf of Demetrius by everyone, and by the truth itself. And we testify as well, and you know that our testimony is true."

"He is very generous."

Gaius went back to the letter and read aloud: "I wrote something to the ecclesia, but Diotrephes, who cherishes preeminence among them, does not receive us. For this reason, if I come, I shall remind you of his deeds, which he enacts while prattling about us with wicked words; and not content with these things, he also does not receive the brothers, and prevents those who would do so, and expels them from the ecclesia."

There was a brief silence. Gaius said, "He has indeed expelled me from his ecclesia. The Lord's Day before last."

All the others stiffened or turned their heads toward him. Titus said, "How foolish he is!"

"We did hear of troubles here. I even worshiped with Diotrephes in better times. What a tragedy!"

Demetrius asked, "Gaius, then where do you worship?"

"Here, in this room."

There was silence for a while, then Agathopodes sighed and spoke. "Do you remember the stories of how some Persian king tied a man's limbs to two different trees that had been pulled down near the earth and then cut the ropes so the trees could spring up? Even so the Body of Christ in this place has been torn apart."

More silence, which Titus broke. "What will you do, Gaius? What *can* you do?"

Gaius frowned and shook his head. "I have been weeping and praying since that Lord's Day, trying to see the way forward. Something Paul wrote floated to the top of my mind. He was writing about divisions within the ecclesia at Corinth. He wrote, 'I planted, Apollos watered, but God gave the increase. So then neither he who plants is anything, nor he who waters, but God who gives the increase.' If I apply that principle here, my task is to let God work in me and through me in this place. This might seem very vague but actually isn't. First, I must embody Christ-like love to all in this place, including pagans and heretics. Second, I must live the true Gospel by worshiping, teaching, and remaining integrated into the Body of Christ, His Ecclesia."

He leaned forward and in a low voice said, "This is a daunting prospect. I cannot hope for quick results or immediate resolution of the separation. The task like improving farmland and growing crops. It takes decades, and there are years of famine and years of bounty. I question whether I can stay the course. Perhaps I would serve God better elsewhere."

Gaius stood at the bottom of the porch stairs, watching the quiet, purposeful bustling as the five missionaries rechecked sandal straps and packs. He embraced each, tears in his eyes, with aching heart. The last was Demetrius. They embraced and exchanged the kiss of peace.

Demetrius said, "Pray for us, brother, and pray for those whom we will meet on the way."

Gaius shifted uneasily from foot to foot, then said "Wait here." He bolted inside. Those gathered looked at each other, wondering at Gaius's odd behavior. Then Gaius ran from the house, carrying a cloak and sack, and said, "Demetrius, I am coming with you."

Demetrius looked confusedly first at his companions, then at Gaius, then at Phocas standing at the door of the house, then back at Gaius. "But what of your household and goods? And what of the ecclesia here?"

Then he walked to Gaius and grasped his upper arms, holding him at arm's length, staring into his face. "Brother, to abandon all and come with us is truly a Christ-like action, and I bless you for your resolve. It is to die in an instant to all these things here." He stepped back and with a wave indicated the house and buildings.

"But sometimes our dying is not quick, like that of Stephen, but takes years, like that of Paul. In this place you are a bulwark against Diotrephes, a foundation stone upon which the edifice of faith in this place can be built. A bridge is a grand edifice, beautiful and strong. But its pillars stand on the plinth, invisible and unthought of, far under the river's surface. The foundation must withstand the never ceasing action of the waves and currents, else the bridge falls. I fear you are called to stay here and die slowly, my friend."

Gaius stared at Demetrius, then his shoulders drooped and his gaze dropped. He let go his cloak and pack, which fell to the ground. "You are too wise for one so young, Demetrius. But what you tell me I in truth already know." He raised his gaze again to Demetrius's face. "This is indeed where I am to take up my cross."

He and Demetrius again embraced, then Demetrius turned and started down the path. The others also turned and started to walk. As they disappeared around the bend, Demetrius turned, waved, and was gone.

Phocas went back inside. Gaius stood still for a long time, then picked up his cloak and bag and trudged back to the house.

One day many years later Niobe's daughter Euphemia brought a young visitor to Gaius. Now well along in years, he was reclining on a kline set up in the open courtyard, dozing in the warm sunlight. Euphemia's voice had almost a laugh in it as she said, "Here's a visitor. He claims his name is Gaius." Gaius beckoned the young man to sit and asked Euphemia to bring wine and water.

"Well, young man, where are you from, where are you going, and how did you come to be called by the august and revered name of Gaius?" he asked, chuckling.

"Well, sir, you may remember my father Demetrius, to whom you gave hospitality some years ago. He and four others were on their way to Armenia."

"Certainly I remember him! A fine young man, brave and wise. So he named you Gaius."

"Yes, after you. He always told me about your dedication, and that being quietly steadfast is often harder and more valuable than some brief, glorious action."

Gaius couldn't speak and looked away. He was saved from embarrassment by Euphemia's arrival with the wine and water. Gaius and Gaius talked until well after the sun set and the courtyard grew dim.

[*Whatever historical truth there is in the words I put into Diotrophes's mouth comes from Larry Hurtado, Lord Jesus Christ: Devotion to Jesus in Earliest Christianity, chapter 6, the section "The Christological Crisis in Johannine Christianity" Wm. B. Eerdmans Publishing Co. Obviously Hurtado is not responsible for my renderings or rendings of things he wrote.*

Bible quotations are generally from the New King James Version, Thomas Nelson.]

~ THE LIGHT ~

THE MERMAIDS DANCE

By Aquarius Denimore

I have always loved the ocean. My favourite place to be. So when I came upon the will leaving the big house on the cliff in Rhode Island to me, I was overjoyed.

I had always loved that big house, the house my mother would tell me stories about. She would put me to bed weaving her tales of how when she was a little girl her mother would take her to visit her grandmother there. She said it was a magical place, a place of wondrous magical beings that no-one else could see, except for those who could see with there mind and their heart. She told me how she would often look out of the widows walk at the top of the house, staring at the ocean and could feel she was being stared at. She could see them in the distance, in the sea as they leapt up out of it from time to time. Always singing a beautiful sirens song, beckoning her into their world.

The day finally arrived for me to move into the big house. I took very few belongings with me as I knew I already loved the old style of furnishings that my great grandmother had, most still in great shape, others which had been lovingly restored. I moved the last box in and was preparing my dinner, when I looked out at the sea I could tell there was a horrible storm on its way. I finished cooking and ate my salmon and rice.

As I finished and went to clean the dishes, the lights began to flicker. I knew it wouldn't be long before I was sitting in the dark in the big old house all by myself. I looked around frantically for any type of lighting I could find. Candles, flashlights, lanterns.

I found plenty of candles but no matches to be found. Flashlight? No. But I did find an old lantern in the back of one of the cupboards. It wasn't from my great grandmothers time, probably not even my grandmothers. It was newer than that and it used batteries.

Now, to find batteries for it. I looked around everywhere I could in the kitchen to try to find them, with no luck. Well, I surmised, I will just have to look around the house. I looked high and low going into every room.

Finally I was at the last room and was hoping I would finally find batteries here. When I went to open the door it was locked. Strange, I thought, why would there be a door locked in the house? I looked around for a key but could find none when suddenly the lights went out. Oh no! I thought, as I was all alone, in the darkness. I became frightened and was looking for a way to any light I could find when I heard the most beautiful singing I had ever heard coming from the other side of the locked door. I could also see light emanating from the room behind the door. I stood there transfixed on the door and the beautiful voices when the door flung open on its own accord.

I walked into the room. The lights were incredible! Pink and purple and blue and green, flashing all around me while the soft white glowed. It was so beautiful I wanted to stay here forever. I caught a slight glimpse of the mermaids dancing around the lights, singing. They were exquisite creatures. Long, blonde, flowing hair like moonbeams in the night sky. They called to me to dance their dance, to enter their world with them as an invited guest along for the ride. I got up and danced with them and sang their song and I never felt more alive, more connected than I did at that moment.

Time passed and I awoke, my head lying on the desk of the study. I looked around for the mermaids but there were none. I shook my head and said to myself of course there are no mermaids, you were dreaming. I got up to go and when I looked down on the floor, I saw the ocean, and the mermaids swimming by, waving to me, still calling to me as they do to this very day. I always want to go dance their magical dance with them.

CITY OF PANKHURST

by Hannah 4242

Her face hit the sand as her knees grazed across the smaller sharp stones that lay just at the entrance to the city, the gates starting to shut quickly behind her. She jumped to her feet, wincing in pain as she saw the cuts on her knees. She fought back the tears and shouted up at the wall. No answer. She picked up a rock and was about to throw it when a voice called down.

"What do you want?"

Looking up she saw a guard on the upper part of the wall, just a head from her angle but she recognized the face immediately. Emma, she had gone to class with her.

"Emma. There's been some mistake, it's me, let me back in." She called up

Emma's face disappeared from over the wall. She shouted again and was contemplating throwing the rock again when Emma appeared from one of the lower balconies on the wall.

"I know who and what you are." She shouted down matter of factly. "There's been no mistake, I saw your trial, you're lucky it was just exile. Your mother pulled some strings for you."

Trial....what trial, she didn't remember any trial. Just two arms wrapped around hers, thrown in a cell with cuffs on, then a few hours later being roughly thrown out the entrance just now.

"What trial?" she finally asked as Emma stared down at her.

"You know what trial. I know the truth. To believe I was your friend. I can't believe you wouldn't tell me. I was your friend"

"The truth ... .tricked you? What's going on?"

Emma watched unmoving like a statute judging her

"A trial, exile … .wait that can't mean … .you can seriously believe that…" she stammered and trailed off, finally starting to understand what was happening.

"Emma. You know me. I'm not, we did sports at school together. You know I can't be…"

"A man" Emma spat down. "I saw you, at the rite, you beat that other man senseless."

"What does that prove? Ascension Rite? I was proving I could protect you all."

"You just proved what I'd suspected for years. You're a man, dangerous and violent. Your kind aren't allowed here, it's bad enough you tricked us all for so long. I trusted you, and you didn't have the guts to tell me at all."

A tear started to form in Emma's eyes. "Go, and don't come back."

"Emma, I…" She stammered again, stepping forward.

A bolt buried itself in the ground just in front of her.

"No more warnings" Emma hissed as she showed the end of a now empty crossbow just over the balcony wall. "Any closer and I will have to shoot you"

She froze looking at the bolt sticking in the ground. She thought quickly, she knew from royal tours of the walls that guards wouldn't even bother with warnings normally.

"Emma, please, it's me. This isn't right, and you know it."

Another older guardswoman that she didn't recognise stepped up behind Emma.

"You are right," The woman called down

She breathed a sigh of relief that someone saw sense at last.

"Here" the older guard shouted as the doors slid open a crack and a leather bag got thrown out. "Your supplies as required by law. We aren't monsters like you. Now go before I order my guards to fend off an attack by a wandering man"

She leaned over carefully and grabbed the bag by the handle, knowing she had no choice. She could feel the confusion and anger welling up inside her. She wanted to throw the rock. Aim for the older woman's head. She sighed, but who would she be defending then? Plus she'd not even get to throw it, there was bound to be more bolts trained on her. She continued to fight back the tears, she didn't want to let them see her so weak but as she turned and walked away, she couldn't hold back the tears any longer.

PARTNERS IN CRIME

by Trinny Mizin

Gigino scratched his groin and his manacles clinked noisily. The guards had done their best to restrain the Gnome with chains that were fitted for people of twice his stature. After much tugging and swearing they'd eventually given up on trying to get him into the leg manacles. He found, that if he stood on the stone bench then he had a reasonable degree of freedom with his arms. His itchy head was his next priority. Several creatures were dislodged by his efforts and he watched mournfully as they made a bid for freedom down the grate in the centre of the cell.

He missed his backpack. 'We'll need that for evidence' the guard had said before dragging him off to his cell. Peddling without a license. Whoever thought of such a stupid crime! It wasn't like it cost the little coastal town anything to have him there on a street corner selling his toys and gadgets. It was trade rules again. Trade rules had driven him from his home in Rocksbottom all those years ago. And weapons, he recalled. Large heavy spiky weapons and the threat of them being used against small squishy Gnomes. And here he was again, with humans telling him what to do and robbing him of both his liberty and his backpack.

"Can't stand humans!" He said and then sat there trying to remember if he'd said it out loud. He quite liked some humans; it was just that others often seemed to pick on him.

The cells only other occupant was barely visible under a mass of chains. All morning she had been snoring steadily punctuated by the occasional growl. Gigino became aware that the noise had subsided and she was regarding him with suspicion through one open eye.

"Oh, you're awake." Said Gigino, trying to sound friendly.

"Really, I was rather hoping I wasn't." She retorted while taking in her surroundings.

"I'm Gigino." Offered the Gnome. "And you are?"

"I'm Lillith." Despite being trussed up like a mummy in chain she struggled until she was upright. She swallowed and took the deepest breath she could, given the constriction of her bonds. "And I've got a stinking hangover."

The jailer with the hunchback and one eye (every dungeon has one) leered at the pair through the bars in the door. His eye widened when he saw that Lillith was awake and he immediately scampered off towards the guardhouse. "Lillith ith awake. Fetch the thargant! Lillith ith awake!" (Lillith was actually the first prisoner ever who's name he could adequately pronounce).

Sergeant Scales was a mean man who enjoyed his job. The two guards who accompanied him had been present at the 'arrest' and one of them still seemed to be having problems walking.
"Prisoner Lillith will stand while the charges are read out." Scales announced. He laughed in the hope that the other guards would join him. Much to his surprise Lillith stood up. The uninjured guard sniggered for a moment before being silenced by a glance from his boss.
"It's quite a list isn't it? Three counts of murder, forty eight counts of manslaughter, thirty six counts of damage to private property, three counts of damage to public property, forty five counts of malicious wounding, one hundred and six counts of grievous wounding." He stopped to take breath in that 'we've really got you bang to rights this time sunshine' way of all coppers. "Two hundred and fifty seven counts of miscellaneous wounding and seven counts of brawling in a public place."

"I'm sure it was only one brawl." Lillith explained. "I mean I'm a little hazy on the details but I'm sure it was only one."

"Then why," Said Scales, waving the charge sheets under her nose. "Have I got reports from several times in the evening?"

"It was a very long brawl." She considered this. "Mind you, now you come to mention it I do remember stopping for a burger at one point."

"I don't think you fully understand the magnitude of the trouble you're in Lillith. I really haven't the time for all the paperwork on this one and neither has the court. His lordship can get really ratty if he misses his early afternoon nap. I've decided to present all of your crimes as one charge of genocide. How do you feel about that Lillith?"

"Proud."

"Excuse me sir." Said the upright guard. "You didn't mention the crime of kicking Constable Coggs in the privates."

"I think you'll find that particular misdemeanour under miscellaneous wounding."

"Begging sir's pardon sir." Interjected Constable Coggs.

"Yes what is it Constable?"

"It was malicious woundin sir. I remember finkin at the time that wot she did to my goolies was right malicious. I remember finkin sir, that's going in my report that is. I mean, given the choice I'd ave preferred it if something a little more miscellaneous ad appened to me tackle."

"Yes Constable, thank you Constable. I've read your report." Said Scales irritably.

"I mean it could ave been grievous sir. Only what with the booze and her bein right knackered she just collapsed before me bulgin eyes. I suppose she ad ad a bit of a night of it. But I was finkin sir..."

Scales had been quietly seething at the persistence of his subordinate "Were you indeed?"

"...I mean, wot if it ad ave been grievous woundin sir? Ow would I ave told the wife? Anyow it's all in my report sir. About ow it really urt and everyfink."

"Constable, I'm sure we all sympathise with the unfortunate condition of your testicles"

"Ha ha." Said Gigino. "Could have been serious, could have been a charge of genitalocide!"

The occupants of the cell regarded the chuckling gnome blankly.

"Everyone finks it's funny." The Constable mumbled.

Scales regarded Lillith, as a spider may regard its victim within a cocoon. "If I'm not very much mistaken you'll be hanged by your pretty little neck until dead come the morrow." He leaned closer. "And that will give us all something to think about, won't it? Mark me Lillith, you shall pay for your crimes."

"Dead or alive, Scales. I regret what I choose to. If a man draws a sword on me then that gives me the right to kill him. They could have put their swords down and left it, they didn't. Whose fault is that?"

"I was thinking." Said Gigino, after the three had left. Lillith was silently contemplating her imminent demise and ignored him. "They're not going to want to take those chains off until after they hang you, on account of you hitting them and escaping and such. And that chain seems much attracted to that mysterious force known as gravity."

"Gnome, do you have a point or can I go back to contemplating these matters without your help?"

"Oh yes, I was just pondering whether I should attempt to broker a deal with you. What warrior code do you follow?"

"I would not reveal that to a Gnome. What would such as you know of the code?"

"Oh, enough to get by." He retorted smugly as he inspected his grubby fingernails. "I expect you could probably be persuaded to swear on that code if you were to find yourself in a bit of a pinch."
"I would never swear upon my code to a Gnome."

"Oh well, suit yourself. Stay here and mope and have your head pulled off in the morning if you like."

With that Gigino sat down and thrust three fingers up his left nostril. (Do not try this at home! Special gnome size nostrils are required for this feat.)

"Well isn't that just Gnomes for you?" Sneered Lillith. "Find themselves in a tight spot and they sit and pick their nose." Gigino carefully withdrew a set of lock picks and set about undoing his manacles. "Gnome, you mentioned a deal."

"I have a name you know." Now Lillith really was in trouble. She'd never had to remember a name before. 'Oi you!' had always got her by in life up until now. When Gigino was out of his manacles he padded up to the door and looked under it. The corridor beyond seemed sufficiently clear of guards. In moments it was open and he crept out leaving Lillith to consider her fate. Suffer a nasty death or learn to be polite to people. Life offered some hard choices when you didn't have a sword in your hand. There was a click as Gigino locked the door behind him.

He peeped under the next door he came to. "Hello Bozzy, how are you doing?" The three scruffy youths looked up to see where the voice was coming from. There was a large nose clearly visible under their cell door.

"Oh ello Gigin." Gigin... Gigino, thought Lillith. She repeated it to herself, trying to remember it. "Been feeling a bit down now you come to mention it. We got arrested you know."

"Really, I was wondering what you were doing in here." Said Gigino distractedly. "How did you get caught?"

"Long story mate. We were robbin Gaudman's, you know that jewelers down Silver street."

"Oh I know it. I was casing that place up a couple of weeks ago. I hope you spotted the mace trap just over the door." Scabs, in addition to his more general injuries, now had a large lump on his forehead. "Ah," Said Gigino. "Anyway, I remember seeing a couple of hooks on the bottom of two display cases and thinking 'I bet he has a tripwire across them at night' I reckoned he had a crossbow set up just behind his window display cases."

"He did." Said Mucker flatly. His pride and left buttock were still smarting from the memory of it.

"And the foot cantrips, the ones under the carpet behind the rope barrier by his main display case?"

"What were you after pinching?" Asked Bozzy. The long limp up to the dungeon after their arrest was not something he cared to recall.

"Oh I had my eye on his tools. You wouldn't believe how good jewelery maker's tools are."

Bozzy was a simple crook, with a clear view of his own priorities. "That place is worth a fortune Gigin. I can't believe you'd rob it for a set of tools."

"Oh you never know when a set of tools might come in handy." There was a click and Gigino slipped into the room. Quickly he locked it behind him and sat down with the other three. He draped some spare manacles over himself.

He had heard the jailer doing his rounds, spitting and leering. He was good at his job and it suited his attention span.

He leered through the door's little barred window and spat at Scabs. Then the one eye came to rest on Gigino.

"You were in the other thell."

"No I wasn't, couldn't possibly have been, what with being locked up in here and everything. I would have thought a clever jailer such as yourself would have spotted that straight away."

"Yeth, right." Said the jailer, who scratched his head for a moment and ambled off in the direction of Lillith's cell looking forward to a good leer.

"Have you got a plan then?" Asked Bozzy, still lamenting the fact that he hadn't just a few fateful days before.

"Well I haven't yet but I'm working on one. You know that big barbarian woman who arrived five days ago?"

"You mean the one with the great big..."

"Yeah, that's the one."

"I know who you mean, calls herself Lillith." Said Mucker. "She worries me that one. And there's not a great many as I'd say that of."

"Well she's chained up nice and tight in my cell. And I was thinking, what with the guards being scared to death of her and everything..."

"Gigino!" The cry from the adjacent cell was music to his ears.

"Like I say lads, I'm working on it." Gigino made his way back to his cell unlocking and re-locking the doors as he went. He did this under the nose of the jailer whose concentration was entirely focused on a prolonged leer.

Eventually he seemed to register the re-appearance of the gnome and seemed to be having problems patching events together.

"You unlock the door." He said, after much consideration.

"Oh no, wasn't me, couldn't possibly have been me."

"Why not?" He ventured.

"You've got the keys."

"Yeah." Said the jailer and jangled them, just to be on the safe side. "I got the keys." He continued on his rounds.

"You were saying, my dear." Smugness oozed from every pore as Gigino addressed the helpless woman.

"What sort of oath were you hoping I might swear?"

"One of partnership."

"Partnership?"

"Yes, as I see it we both have certain skills. I can liberate you from your bonds and then you can go and explain to the guards how uncomfortable you found them. Which, I think, may largely sort out our present conundrum. In the long term however, there will be immense benefits for both of us, I'm sure."

"Do you really think that I would enter into a partnership with a Gnome?"

"No I don't. I expect that pride will get the better of you and you'll have an unwelcome addition to your necklace collection tomorrow. I bet you'll wish you were in a partnership though, when they bring you your last meal and you've got nobody to spoon feed it to you."

"I shall swear this oath." Said Lillith, through gritted teeth.

"How's it going in there Gigin?" Shouted Bozzy.

"Very well. I think the chains will be coming off pretty soon."

"Can I watch?" Said Scabs, before he could stop himself.

"So we're partners." Continued Gigino. "Yes?"

"To this I swear." Lillith wasn't stupid. It was just that, given her other skills, she didn't need to be clever that often.

Gigino started working on the first padlock. "And you're not to hurt my friends either. Scabs tends to drool a lot when he's in female company but you're not to let it bother you alright?"

"Alright. And this partnership, it doesn't mean you're expecting to order me around does it?"

"Of course it does and you can order me around. We don't have to do what the other says but we do have to listen. You know, a partnership." She didn't know, but resigned herself to giving it a try.

Lillith arose. Her muscles flexed and her biceps shone and that bit on her bum where the chain was digging in was starting to feel a lot better. Gods she's ugly Gigino thought. She's much too tall and, while big, isn't nearly fat enough. "I'm off to let the lads free and see who else they've got in here. You get the life back into your limbs and I'll be back soon."

As Lillith stretched herself she could hear Gigino, some way down the corridor explaining to the jailer why he couldn't possibly be running around the dungeon freeing people. "Oh and Lillith was just asking me where that handsome jailer is. You know, I think she fancies you."

Lillith smiled sweetly when a set of disfigured, but hopeful, features appeared at the window. She kicked the door so hard that it was torn off its hinges, pinning the unfortunate jailer against the opposite wall with his head wedged between the bars. "Thank you." She said as she took his keys. She briefly considered spitting on him but was afraid he might take it the wrong way.

And so, the many miscreants of Seaweed Bay assembled and advanced on the guardhouse with Lillith in the lead. There was only one constable on duty. He had been relieved of his patrol duties for the day on account of a very painful injury he had sustained in the course of duty.

"I will do, worrever you ask." Said Constable Coggs in that mechanical way of the truly terrified.
"Except, maybe, if we ask you to stand with your eyes closed and your legs open." Mused Gigino.
"Where's my backpack?"

"And my sword." Said Lillith. This was chorused with additional requests from the assembled throng.

"It's all in there." The frightened constable pointed out a door opposite.

There was a loud "Ouch!" From the room beyond, Sergeant Scales was learning that no one but Gigino should attempt to open his backpack without a complex set of instructions and a hefty pair of gauntlets.

Lillith burst into the room and kicked Scales' guard in the back of the head. As he went down she swept up her sword from a nearby bench. Scales took a moment to free himself from the Backpack and by the time he looked up he was facing Lillith down the length of her sword. She raised it.

"Hold on!" Said Gigino.

"Why?"

"Well, you know how it is? Commit a crime and it's paperwork. Kill a guard and it's personal."

"Then what are we going to do with him?"

"I want to go to Bridgecrossing." Said Lillith as the pair walked along the beach. She was pleased to be away from Gigino's friends. She didn't mind being worshipped. It was being drooled over that she objected to. They had to leave. There were already rumors of an army being raised to re-capture her.

"We don't want to go there." Bridgecrossing was very unfriendly to gnomes. "We ought to go to Freehaven. You know, big town, lay low for a bit."

"They'll have got him down now. I'm not saying that stripping him naked and running him up a flagpole wasn't a good idea but the next watch will have rescued him already."

"This is it you see, he' ll have to be rescued. We undermined his authority. Believe me, It will hurt him more than a swift kick in the Coggs' ."

And so the pair went to Freehaven, via Bridgecrossing. Where, incidentally, they are a lot more polite to Gnomes than they used to be.

MYMO

by Soen Eber

Violet's Dream

Vi felt herself ascending.

She gave a kick of her legs, arms thrusting. The glow in the water above her was growing larger and brighter.

She would be surfacing soon. Her respirator made gurgling noises, as bubbles rose above her in a swaying motion. Watching the rising column, their noises lowered in pitch, becoming -

gentle snoring?

She sunk deeper, light dimming; the noises receding to a hushed low background pitch and then fading.

A distant noise crashed upon her again, stirring her slightly. Soft pale light leaked through the window, with the sound of far-off storms washing themselves against it in a constant rumble. "No accident," she thought, "that ancient Greeks heard Zeus in their evening and early morning thunder, for the sea breezes would lift moisture high above the land, only to condense and slide back into the sea."

That sudden burst of rationality lifted her away from unbroken temples, away from the cloud-shorn mountains of Olympus.

"There's that snoring again", she remembered. Consciousness welling up, her eyes flickered. It was indeed early morning. Their was faded light from the window. Her eyes drifted to the clock: even the birds hadn't awoken; for humans there were only fifteen minutes yet to go. Well, this human, anyways.

She envied them. Far more sensible, they did not place themselves under the strictures of imposed, unnatural schedules.

That flash of instinct to the clock had voided her awareness of a warm, unfamiliar yet comforting presence in the bed next to her. It was attached to an arm. His arm, where he had draped it upon her as they slept. From her side, a faint, soft snore issued.

She had found the source.

Mymo, her pet human and childhood friend. What was he doing in her bed, and not on the floor or in is basket in the den? She would have to do something about that.

Eventually.

But it was nice, so very very nice having him there, where he was. Her thoughts raced, however, banishing future rest for the morning.

If only he had a steady job. If only they weren't in a three person flat shared by two other women, her bestest friends from Uni. One must have standards after all, for Mymo was a freeloader, a friend with a convincing sob story to let him stay with them, despite the flat's full occupancy and the absent owner's strict "no men" policy. His daughter, Astra, one of her flat mates, was generous enough to share it with a few, good friends. An investment of her father's within which Astra and her closest female friends could use so she would have a home with pleasant company. A base in London for future ventures, if she chose to keep it.

And she had a lot of friends. Vi was lucky to be among them.

So Mymo was her pet and live-in helpmate, her only condition for taking him in as remembrance for their childhood games. She as a circus ringmaster, he as a roaring lion or some other great intrepid animal. She even still had her sister's hulu hoop which was a part of their games, remembering Mymo jumping through it to her great applause.

There were other conditions. They would have to hide Mymo's presence from her father, or at least his maleness. Malcolm Davies (no relation) would not have a man living with his daughter unless he bore her a ring, and Mymo had a scant few of those qualities for which that man would yet accept.

The other condition was Mymo would be everyone's pet and maid, not just Vi's.

Mymo, with his slim, graceful build and theatre background, would make a convincing woman with the right help, and carried a fine feminine voice which he could affect so long as it was not strained from overuse. He would pass, if everyone was careful.

It was temporary, so very temporary.

She glanced at his perforced girdle which hung over a chair, its padded breast forms and buttocks secured with pink and yellow laces and a firm elastic. Even with his optimistic and sunny disposition, she was certain he hated it. But it was central London, they had found a home here, among friends. He was close to theatres where he could find work, once he got lucky and / or the recession kicked over, and for Vi she was close to work, in Portcullis House on WestMinister, their offices near to the House of Commons. Traffic, be not proud. She would not go quietly into her former commute.

But again, there must be standards. He had also cost her 15 minutes of sleep and with her mind racing she would not be able rest for even those few moments.

So Vi raised an elbow, and in a swift calculated motion - not meant to cause pain but enough to get the job done, she pushed and forced her friend Mymo to fall in a tangled heap to the floor, taking the blankets with him.

Regrettable. She needed those blankets.

"Ugh."

"Huh?", she groaned sleepily, peeping over. "Mymo! What are you doing here?" she said, feigning surprise.

Vi had already worked it out. She had kipped it early to get a good start on the next day, things to take care of and all that. The others were partying, celebrating … something of Marci's, probably her website, but it hadn't caused any "tired and emotional" lack of sleep. "Even with this lot, such is not impossible", she thought, smiling. "… but for now all is sorted right and proper."

Good.

It was good. But there would be consequences. Astra had some bloody good vintages lying about, her father being a bit of a wine snob. An occupational hazard, being on the Arts Council. Inattention was inevitable, and Mymo invading her bed by accident was one of those consequences. His being latched in by his collar into a cat costume, hands in mitts, fluffy ears and all meowing with surprise was the other.

He could not get into, or out of the costume. Not without help.

He meowed again, piteously, his legs shaking and squirming after he'd seated himself upright.

"Speak", she said, aware of the house rule that did not permit him to do so while so costumed, or told not to while collared. It was, sometimes, the only way to get some peaceable quietude on those occasions on which he was feeling jazzed. Which was often.

"I, ah ..." he sputtered.

Great, she thought, what a time for him to be at a loss of words.

"NOW". She was nonplussed. Still more stuttering.

"OK," Vi responded. "It's obvious either Marci or Astra locked you in your costume, and by the "girl code" I cannot release you. So which one was it?" she asked.

Mymo remained silent, turning his head left and right, glancing around; his legs still trembling.

No, she had worked it out. He was squirming. He had to pee.

"Alright," Vi said. "It's commendable you're not going to rat anyone out, but I did not put the collar on you, and so you are going to have to be the one who asks whoever put this on you to take it off. And quickly, I'm not about to have you pee on the floor."

He meowed again, louder.

"Don't look this way, Mymo. Turn yourself around properly so I can get a good look at you, and then scamper off, tails up!" Vi almost giggled as she said the latter, and then giggled for real when she changed her mind. She jumped out of bed and grabbed his tail. He had stolen her blankets after all.

She broke out laughing, shouting "Too Cute!" repeatedly, dragging poor Mymo by the tail behind her on the bedroom's polished cedar floor. She headed towards the door to the hallway, beyond which the others' apartment lied. "Get thee hence!" she shouted. All he could do now was meow piteously and constantly as she pulled on him, making her laugh even louder. Fortunately, Marci had reinforced that appendage, anticipating future use.

Marci was evil.   Twice evil, for having also sewn the formerly detachable paws onto the costume.   The thought made Vi snort loudly. He was such great fun this way.

Mymo sat semi-akimbo in the hallway outside Astra and Marci's bedroom. He thought for a moment he should only merely lean with the back of his head and shoulders against the door, and wait for one of them to get up. He could hold it from the last night if they woke on time.

Testing, he held his hand up to knock while still sitting, but the sight of the fur-clad paw stayed him. "Faux fur", he thought to himself, adding "I shouldn't" more urgently. He was still in pet animal mode.

Lowering his paw he instead listened quietly, hoping for signs of movement from Vi's earlier giggle-fit having awoken them.

"Let Vi take the blame," he thought to himself, crossing his arms in front. The thought stilled him even further, continuing: "I am rather vulnerable here." He felt his back shiver, knocking against the door. He willed himself to stillness, and the vibration halted.

Another moment, and he let his breath out. No sound of movement. He sat there, leaning without movement, for some while.

With some relief he heard their alarms go off, the steady drone of Astra's BBC announcer reading the news intermingling with Marci's Radio 2 "Music in the Morning", low and softly. He was listening through the door: he heard the words "scandal" and the name of the MP for whom Vi worked.

Vi had warned him off waking them early for whatever reason when he first came to her, noting the two had a furious streak to their vengeance about such things. Nothing harmful or malicious, just that he would be better off otherwise, she said, without going much into further detail.

It was much worse now, his need to go. Sleep was no longer dulling that part of his brain.

A couple of minutes later, the door opened: Astra appeared full-fluff in her pyjamas and toothbrush. She gave a little yelp as he almost toppled into her legs, but he caught himself in time. "Dancer's reflexes", he sighed internally.

"Mymo, what ..?!?" she said, surprise writ on her face. She quickly recovered, however, turning her head and speaking loudly: "Marci, your little friend is here, come see what he wants." Looking down again, her face showed a slight touch of irritation even as she let out a soft "Awwww". She reached down to pat him on the head. But she let her irritation show by the death lock her fingers had on his hair, pulling at it slightly in warning. "I'm afraid I haven't woken up yet. Sorry little neko boy, it's still too early for your antics." Mymo might have only imagined the "for your antics" part, but it was evident in her tone. She tugged menacingly again on his long, ginger, curly locks. A bare, muttered whisper-passing her lips: "Of course he's a ginger."

"Marci, hurry up." Mymo heard a distant groan, and then the rustle of bed-things. He saw the arm of a red, pink, purple and teal paisley robe hurriedly whipping about, and an accompanying arm struggling to find it's new home. "No," he said internally when he saw her in a better light: "Scarlet, magenta and heliotrope. Yay for bFA" he deadpanned only to himself. The teal was still teal, however.

Marci rubbed her eyes, wearing a confused expression. Mymo whined, puppy-like before switching back to meowing, his face pointing off-canter towards the hallway before looking up at them again. His meow was louder this time.

"What's up, girl, why the long face?" Astra asked, getting a dig in at Mymo as she had quickly picked up on his out-of-character whine. He was supposed to be a cat after all. It also caused Marci to ask "What, is he, a dog or a cat? I know I left a neko boy downstairs when I went to bed, I checked," she smirked. "Vi! What did you bring home?", she shouted, turning her head down the hallway.

Mymo blinked in awareness, they were awful quick on the pickup to only have woken up. It may have been Vi had awoken them after all, which meant the two before him had spent their fifteen minutes thinking things out, instead of sleeping. He was doomed.

Mymo meowed again, and, no longer able to suppress his leg motions, he wobbled uncertainly on them, still sitting with his legs crossed.

Astra, ever the fast thinker, caught on instantly. "Marci, you left him in that overnight! How's he supposed to pee?"

"I'm sorry, Mistress, I ... I did what?," she said, still comprehending. Marci wasn't as reflexively fast as Astra, but she was organized and methodical. "That wasn't in the plan!"

"You should have made a list!" Astra said. "You should have expected I'd break out the wine, reaching 100,000 subscribers is a really big deal. You know that!"

Astra bent down again, having never released her hand from his hair. "I'm sorry, Mymo, Marci and I are going to have to work this out so you're just going to have to wait a few more minutes. Something like this could cause a lot of problems if it's not talked out."

Her hand gave a final, harsh tug of his hair, causing him to yip in pain.

Mymo moaned. His legs were still trembling but now his whole body was rocking like some kind of a mechanical wind-up toy.

"Yup, doomed," Mymo thought. His eyes were seeing stars now.

Astra went on: "As primary tenant of this unit, I claim sufficiency for chairing this discussion. Are there any objections?"

"No objections, your honor. May I approach and be recognized?" said Marci.

Mono grunted, nearly doubling over.

"Silence in the court,"said Astra.

Mymo remained still, as much as was possible.

"The party approaching the bench is recognized. You may proceed, Marci." Astra said.

"Your honor: I move that due to a lack of quorum, this decision should be tabled. Mymo is Miss Violet's pet, and being the responsible pet owner she should be present and she is not."

"Overruled," Astra said quickly. "Mymo is sentient and, as a human of non-diminished capacity, of sound mind and sound body, is responsible for his own actions and decisions. To whit: allowing himself to be locked into the catsuit he is currently wearing, with full knowledge that doing so would place him in a capacity of diminished ability to perform bodily functions for a period of several hours without (A), potentially damaging his costume, and (B) potentially damaging the fixtures and furnishings of this unit, for which I am responsible."

"Your honor," Marci said. "I move to void condition (A) of your reasoning: quite well thought out too so may I add - "

"You may. Thank you," interjected Astra.

"Continuing, your honor, I move condition (A) be voided as the catsuit is Mymo's property and, with the understanding that Mymo is allowed to own 'property' even under his diminished role as 'flat pet', this proceeding has no standing in ruling over damages performed to his own property. He may dispose of such to his own preference without prejudice."

There was a moan of agreement, which the two readily ignored save for a mild kick to Mymo's side.

"The condition is so voided, you may continue with your proceeding." said Astra. "Your reasoning is also quite excellent."

"Thank you your honor. I would further note that in his current, distressed condition, he is becoming liable for causing actual, and not merely potential damage, to this unit's floor, structural components, and bathroom furnishings should this debate continue. Further, with our full knowledge of his condition and potential for liability, we ourselves suffer from an incurred liability should we continue and not relieve him of his burden." said Marci.

"So noted," said Astra. "The chair rules this discussion is tabled, and that administrative action should be recommended to the pet's owner to fully remind him of his rights and obligations inside this flat. The discussion is thereby tabled and shall be considered resolved upon performance of said administrative action. The chair so rules. The chair also rules that in the interest of expediency and without objection that while Violet was the actual party who awakened us, responsibility of such devolves to Momo as it was his decision which became the inciting incident for causing her to wake us up in the first place. Are there any objections?"

"No objections, your honor."

"The discussion is so tabled." Astra concluded.

Quickly, Marci unbuckled Mymo's collar and hurriedly undid the long, hidden zipper along his backside, allowing him to egress.. "Go," she said, smiling.

"See, I told you it would only be a few minutes," Astra chuckled to his swiftly departing backside. The bathroom door opened with a bang, causing her to wince. There was a loud clatter of porcelain.

"There will be an inspection afterwards," Astra shouted. "There better not be any damage."

"Don't wake us up again," Marci added.

Mymo bustled himself in the bathroom. He took a quick shower after the necessities, and briefly checked the cat suit for any stains or damage. None were evident so it would only need airing later in the morning, although of course the lining would need to be washed as was normal for extended use. The suit was well constructed, being a theatre costume meant for continued use for a play he had been in. When it closed unexpectedly, it and the rest of the costumes and props were passed on to the performers in lieu of pay, as many were special constructed and not belonging to a prop house.

There was a knock on the door. His ten minutes were up. He should have been wiping down the shower and fixtures instead of inspecting the suit. Dropping it and grabbing a long towel, he hurriedly wiped down the shower and fixtures with it. "Be right out!," he shouted, wrapping the towel around his waist, tucking it in as his other hand grabbed the costume. Astra was waiting outside. Smiling, she reached up to rub his head, saying "right on time, pet, I knocked a minute early figuring you'd be a might bit distracted." She ran her right hand along his cheek, looping his chin with a long fingernail before ending with a slight "boop" as she pressed his nose. "All good now I hope?" He nodded, further opening the door and stepping out of her way. Once inside her blonde head did a quick swivel left and right. She reached out to pull back the shower curtain and behind the door where it had been slammed open. "You did good, pet," she said, smiling again as she closed it, her face filling the gap.

With all the high-end furniture in Astra's luxury owner-occupied flat, normal pets like cats and dogs were out of the question. Mymo filled an unexpected need.

Three women, one Mymo, two bathrooms. Morning rush hour was highly regulated. Mymo was first and fastest, so he could help the others as they prepared for the day, organizing, cleaning, retrieving any necessary stray objects: "step and fetch" as his racist BNP organizing uncle would call it. He was a pet and not a slave, just helping out in any way he could to make things easier for everyone, including himself.   And being a women's pet was far better than being homeless. The terms were agreeable.

He grabbed the girdle (or more properly a bodysuit) which Vi had conveniently left by her door. It was elastic, and, upon reaching the hallway's walk-in closet, he undid the towel to throw on a pair of white panties and a heavier white cotton shift, which he needed to protect skin and girdle from each other. With the ever-present risk of Astra's father Mr. Davies stopping by unannounced as well as the flat's management, service workers, neighbors and visitors, men's clothing could not be around. It was an iron-clad rule.

He took and draped a shirt on his arm before leaving the closet, where he saw Marci waiting for him.

"Oh hey, there you are, I wanted to talk with you; I'm waiting for my turn anyways so this will be a good time," she smiled, steering him by the arm towards the former den/study. The room was totally glassed in, fronting the living room by the hallway and was meant to be a showpiece full of 18th century furniture which Mister Davies had now hid safely in storage, leaving the room empty for the girls to furnish on their own.

The living room itself held Herman Miller chairs and Adrian Pearsall mid-century modern; collector pieces one had to be careful about. Astra had placed some high quality but definitely cheaper furnishings facing them for guests when she moved in. And a cushion for Mymo when he moved in as well, deep, plush & comfortable.

The study, now rechristened "the comfort room", was eclectically furnished, and held a couple of make up tables: one full-bore and the other for quick touchups. There were comfortable chairs and a couch, and a low but stylish wicker basket with cushions and blankets, long enough for a person to comfortably sleep in if they curled up properly.

Mymo had to sleep somewhere, and he was too lanky and too cute to sleep on the uncomfortable high closet shelf he had been originally meant for. They wanted him on display and not moved on as originally intended. Again, none of the girls could have an animal pet, so Mymo filled an unexpected and greatly welcomed opening. He did it quite well.

A Proposal

Marci sat in an overly comfortable leather plush chair which nearly swallowed her, leaving only enough space for her hand to softly wave him to the floor, whereupon he sat, legs spread out and hands touching the floor space in front of him, raising his eyes to meet hers. With his hair not-yet managed, he looked a bit like Edward from Cowboy Bebop.

She was still wearing the paisley robe. "I saw you admiring this," she said.

"I was," he said. "I was working out the colors: scarlet, magenta, heliotrope and teal."

"Rose, not magenta. Magenta is brighter and kind of candy'ish, but yay for working it out," she said. "As a textile artist I have to know this. Boring, yech." She made a face.

She turned slightly. "I swear to God you must have studied 'cute' when you were getting your arts degree," she said, glancing down again and smiling at his posture. "I'm almost about to boop you on the nose," she added. "But only almost, I am way too comfortable at the moment."

She gave a soft, sweet sigh.

"I was in a couple of plays where it was important." Mymo replied, "There was that one romantic comedy where I was required to play both of the leads. It was high concept and a cost saving measure."

"Both? That must have been difficult."

"Yeah, but it was fun," he said as he picked up her foot and started kneading it. Her eyes quirked at his comment, but she sighed again contentedly as he massaged her foot with his deft hands.

"The comedy parts were really well written," he said with a blush. "And the crew was tightly knit, I learned a hell of a lot, it being my first really-real speaking part," he added.

"It was also where I got the girdle, the stage manager gave it to me as a gift." He had to wear it as part of the kit for the female lead. No one would buy it so it stayed in the theatre trunk, when he was forced out of his last flat by his roommates for non-payment.

"I'd say he was signalling," Marci said.

"You think?" said Mymo, giving an annoyed sigh. "Don't worry, I played it safe. I'm for girls only, anyways."

He switched over to the other foot now, continuing to knead her foot.

Marci shifted in her chair, raising herself to a more seated position. "Well," Marci said abruptly, glancing at the time. "I'll have to explore that sometime but now I do have a request. I need a model for my Cirque Couture website and also for a bit of cosplay modelling. I have to admit it will be odd and edgy so you might not like it if you're aiming for a more conventional modelling career. But I can promise to make it a lot of fun if you like. You seem to really get into humiliation – only as an option of course - but I won't be degrading or mean, just odd. I run my own shoots and most of it right now is only selfies, so I'd like to include some couples and men's fashion as well. What do you think?"

She was nervous, and practically breathless from her rapid run-on speech.

"I'd have to think about that and then talk with Miss Vi," he said. "I don't want to do porn or anything like that."

"Don't worry, it's only risque with lots of teasing," she answered. "I don't think either one of us wants to get locked in to something that is so career limiting." She laughed out loud. "Ha ha, I said locked in", teasingly.

Speaking more softly and with more seriousness, she said "Sorry about leaving you like that last night, it was the wine."

"Well, I had some too," he admitted, hanging his head. "But I'll be sure to ask Miss Vi about that, I think it could really work out." he said with a smile.

"Great!", Marci smiled back. "Oh, and don't forget your shirt," she added as Astra approached the door from the hallway.

As she stepped in, she smiled to Marci, saying "Bathroom's all yours, pet" with a cheerful voice. "I meant my pet, sorry." she giggled, her hand raised to her mouth, her cheeks flushed just a tiny little bit. "Mymo, eggs over easy for me, please, but no rashers. Just some toast. With marmalade," she said, brightening, savoring the anticipated orange sweetness. "Oatmeal for Marci and let her garnish it the way she likes, and go ahead and grab whatever else you need for yourself. I think Vi's already in the kitchen, working, so be respectful with her about the noise."

She paused for a moment, continuing: "You can go now, Me and Marci need our contractually-obligated Bechdel moment," she said with a laugh.

"Yes, Miss Astra," he said. He'd been kneeling still, facing her while she talked. He now stood up with a gracious bow and only then walked to the kitchen. "We really need to put a bow on you," Astra gave as an after-shot, with Marci adding "and BELLS!". After he left Marci quietly said to Astra "We will need to instruct him on how to curtsy like a girl," causing them both to giggle.

He pulled on the sheer sleeveless shirt on his way to the kitchen, surprising himself as he hadn't worn it before. There was a full-frontal yellow duck on the shirt's face, and the back held a shot from behind with it swimming, kicking up a mild froth in the water. It was long enough and just barely opaque enough to only cover his panties and nothing else; the girls had picked it out for him. His dancer's body and long, well-toned limbs were on full display.

As he entered the kitchen Vi was at the table, laptop and papers in neat piles as she held her phone to one ear with a look of concentration. Mymo bowed silently, turning after waiting a moment to check for a reaction before starting to put things in order for breakfast. There was no response aside from a slight smile. She was lost in work.

He heard her muttered comments on the phone as Astra's eggs were cooking. He covered the lid to hide the noise and was working on the toast. He also kept an eye on the kitchen timer which he had deliberately set to go off far beyond when he knew the eggs would be done. It would not cause a distraction; he would only just have to be careful with checking the time. He did the same with the instant oats, setting the microwave for 10 minutes, stopping it only when sufficiently done.

As he was setting everything out on the table Vi finished, and after a short pause spoke: "Mymo, come here please and stand behind me to cuddle, I need to feel something warm and familiar."

He hesitated, glancing at the pantry and cupboard when she repeated his name.

He walked over and stood behind her, leaning his hands on her shoulder as he pressed against her back. She pulled his hands down in front of her, saying only "nuzzle my cheek and ears." He complied, rubbing his own cheek and nose against her face, softly rubbing and working his nose to her side so she could feel his warm breath next to her skin. "No tongue!" she said sharply, smiling at his warm breath.

Astra walked in. "So what's up with the office?" she asked Vi. "I heard on the news there was a bit of a dust-up." She looked around, noting the food on the table. "Mymo, where are the fixings for Marci's oatmeal?"

"Oh, sorry Astra, I grabbed him.   Anyways, one of our staff was teasing a girl he knew, and it got a bit out of hand from what I gather," Vi answered. "It got to the point where she started shouting at him to stop it ... he did, but not before a Guardian reporter in the next room popped out to witness it."

"A reporter was loose in the office?" Astra asked with a shock of surprise.

"Yeah," Vi sighed. "She was getting deep background on an issue we're advocating for; I mean she's not the opposition or anything but she is a reporter, she had to touch back with her editor and write it up. It kind of exploded from there with ITV and others grabbing it and running with the story."

Vi was tempted to say "the enemy" instead of "the opposition", but party headquarters were getting rather dogged not to Americanize any disagreements between political parties, taking the high ground and keeping a civil discourse. "And it was the Guardian after all, we're somewhat aligned."

"What they report is also what the Times & the Sun reports, you can't escape the stench of Murdoch. Don't you have a political officer? This should have happened in Fleet Street, not in your offices."

Vi sighed. "Well, damage done, anyways. They do care deeply for each other, just a lover's spat. Which is deadly in a political office. Distracting, anyways."

"You'll have to move him on," Astra said as she walked to the cupboard, pulling out Marci's raisins, some fruit cups and other assorted oatmeal add-ins such as pecans. "You'll need to put the woman on paid leave as well, I hope it works out for her even if she was partly responsible."

"I know, I know ... he was a pretty decent fellow, they both are. But it's out now."

"Fortunately, " Vi added, "well, for us, anyways, the Chancellor's cockup about immigration and those on redundancy payments is sucking out most of the oxygen. Your coverage won't last much longer."

"Yes, but it has the makings of a perfect political circus, doesn't it?" Astra said "Nothing the press loves more than people misbehaving. You'll have to pray to not get a trifecta, if anyone else in labor doffs it and falls head-first into the tip ... labour could be seriously screwed."

Her family's true calling was working in the government on behalf of the arts. Her grand father: a parliamentary under-secretary of state for Arts and Heritage, her great-grand father a full secretary in the department. Thusly steeped in government and politics, Astra knew her stuff. There was even a Lord back in ... when again was that again?

"Yes," Vi said. "It could lose us the election. It could be one, two, many if another pops off soon. We'd look like the party that can't shoot strait and do the responsibility thing. A total write-off. That's what the party chair was telling me just now. He feels sorry for those responsible but ..."

"Alea iactra est," Astra muttered, softly, and then continued: "How's it going to affect the office workflow?" She didn't ask how the rest of the office was handling it, she knew it was a good operation so of course people would suffer. But for the newly-vacant office position she had a plan. "Is it highly skilled work?"

"it's not like the Tory's where the banks and industry and their press can automagically change up the agenda whenever their side gets all caught up with doing wrong," Vi said bitterly. She was still working on the potential consequences, having shelved Astra's question for the nonce.

Vi pulled Mymo gently by the hair, guiding his head to her lap where she began to knead and rub his scalp, playing with his hair in long, curly strands. "Astra you're wrong," she muttered to herself. "Mymo, you're a strawberry blonde, not a ginger even if that's how you seem to act."

She looked up. "No, not particularly, just some basic intelligence and reporting ability. I mean reports reporting, not – you have an idea, don't you?" Vi asked. She wasn't as sharply perceptive as Astra, but again, she was no slouch either.

Mymo grunted softly and contentedly, enjoying his role as stress-reliever-in-chief. He worked up his own version of purring, but Vi made no visible reaction to it other than her massaging taking on an inflexibly gentler quality.

Astra had just finished her breakfast then as Marci entered the room. "Hi hi everyone," she said, before touching her head to Astra's chin in a snuggle. She was rewarded by Astra running her hand along her head, patting her, one arm around Marci's back and shoulder. They broke off as Marci grabbed for the oatmeal and, after adding a few desultory raisins and walnuts with a single scoop of brown sugar, turned again back to the hallway. "Sorry, got something bothering me on the website, gotta fix it," she paused, turning again around to face everyone, smiling. "I'm sure it'll only be a few, but I'm really fixated on it right now and can't say a damn thing otherwise 'cause my mind's racing so much." Smiling, she made a half curtsy and walked back to her and Astra's room, bowl in hand.

 "I think better with food in my hand," she confessed in a soft apologetic voice.

"I better look after her and see if she's alright," said Astra, leaving with a wan smile.

"So that leaves us again," said Vi, "I've got a quick flat administrative-type thing I need to talk to you about." Mymo's eyes widened and his heart raced, she could almost hear it, and she for real did catch his rapid breathing and spreading eyes. "No, no, nothing's wrong, you didn't do anything bad and you're staying with us," she said, calming him down in a hug until his breathing returned to normal. "The girls love you to pieces, she said lowly, and there's been no hint of anything from Astra's dad. He doesn't know about you yet."

Raising her voice back to normal levels, Vi went on: "You're doing alright even with that deer in the headlights look of yours right now. It's kind of scary-cute you ought to know that."

Mymo smiled, and looked up, a question almost on his lips but he thought it better to remain quiet and to let her continue talking.

"Mymo, I know you're frightened you might get kicked out and end up homeless, maybe on the street, maybe in a shelter and I know your family can only take you in for a couple days, they've got their own problems. I should know, I grew up with them too, as neighbors." she said. "Also, I need you to be human for this, no cute distractions, all right?"

Mymo nodded, almost relieved to be returning to a semblance of ordinary ordinariness.

"Anyways," she said, straightening up. "We have four women - three and one in training, and all know or should know how to say 'no' even when it doesn't feel right to say so. You need to know as well. If anything feels uncomfortable here you can - no, let me amend that, you should speak up. The thing of it is, you should have known the downside of being in that neko outfit overnight but you said and did nothing. Why?" she asked.

"Well, at first I was all in for doing it, and you know we were all of us having fun. We were laughing and teasing each other and maybe the wine just got to all our heads. I didn't think it would be like that, leaving it before going to bed, Marci I mean. Astra was like watching and laughing and smiling so everything seemed OK, you know? It all felt warm and good." Mymo said.

"So the alarm bells kicked in only when they both left you?" Vi asked. "Or was it when she put on the collar, locking you in?"

"I did feel a bit worried 'bout the collar, but we were all super giggly at the time an' no one was thinking or saying much, just reacting and laughing and never even thinking it would come to anything to worry about."

"You should have said something then. Just a 'no', and repeat it. You got that? And another thing, the moment you saw the cat suit come out, you should have set some limits, and should have gotten stinky about them if you need to say such things. Understand now?"

"Yes, Miss Vi" he responded.

"You always – always need to think three moves ahead, especially when you're all comfy since your guard is down then. As a woman, or as a vulnerable pet or anything else, when there are drugs – always you need to be in control. You can't shut that off – no free passes because you're a man, not when you make yourself vulnerable like you did."

Mymo looked down, with disturbing new thoughts in his mind. "I'm going to have to always be careful, aren't I?"

"I'm afraid so, even in safe spaces when drinking is involved. Damn it Mymo, I know you know, being so thin and willowy with your soft features, and training as a performer and dancer of all things. You've told me before you had to be careful sometimes because of people making assumptions."

"I'm still a man, though." he said sullenly.

"Perception trumps that. You don't get to be watchful only some of the time, you have to do it full time especially when the environment is clue bombing you, like alcohol or when you are feeling tired. Learn the triggers – the early ones I mean, when it needs to go to high alert and you still have some control."

She lowered her voice, and gently said, smiling: "Get there first, that is all".

"It did seem Astra and Marci, if they're always three moves ahead as you say ..." He paused and bit his lower lip. "were saying something sub-context, beyond the obvious I mean," Mymo said.

"They were probably horrified when they understood what happened," said Vi. "They haven't said much, just a few things, but I gather they realized how valuable this would be as a training exercise. You still carry around some maleness but hide it for the sake of getting along here, and you're not used to being constantly vulnerable yet." She paused for a moment in thought.

"You need to be more –" she paused, looking for the right word. "frissonable," she settled on. "And you were responsible for waking them up. I'd warned you about that," Vi said, smiling.

Almost as if on cue, Astra reentered the kitchen, and was dressed professionally, carrying her laptop bag and clutch as she was ready to leave.

"I have a client meeting at nine, but I did want to swing around again and touch base on what we were talking about. You've had your 'administrative action', I assume?" She noticed Mymo looking especially quiet and thoughtful. "Good," she said. "Mymo, I'm sorry this morning came as a surprise, but Marci and I talked it through and thought it was needed. I'm glad it worked out."

Mymo tilted his head up, following Astra's words.

Astra concluded: "If you have to learn, do it safely. And it was fun."

She gave it a beat. "Well, for us, anyways."

Another beat.

"For me and Marci, that is." she finished with a twisted grin.

Astra paused again, facing Violet.

"Vi, about that office incident of yours, Can you make a temporary placement recommendation until they can infill the position? Work has to be done, you know, even if some of it goes by the board for a bit." she asked.

"Sure, I suppose so, it would mean more work for me but that was already baked in. It always is," she said, flatly with a sour expression.

"Did you have someone in mind?" Vi asked.

Astra leaned forward, as if launching something: "Mymo here needs a bit of money coming in, aside from what he makes at Streets. I don't mind him living here with us for the moment," she said.

"After all, Boris Johnson has been living in my head rent-free for way too long and at least Mymo is cute and I can scratch him behind the ears."

Smiling, she reached out to do just that, but Vi was already lifting him up by his underarms as if to proudly show him off. Mymo picked up on the cue, and intentionally went all slack and non-resistant, emphasizing the cat-like or rag doll-like pose Vi was trying to make him affect.

"Mymo, you are such a tease," Astra said. What do you say, are you in for it?"

He raised his hand as if to inspect it, curling and facing it into himself. Glancing at Vi and seeing her smile, he said "I've turned my body into an instrument, a work of art, even. I don't know if I'd be very comfortable sitting all the time, Miss Astra, Miss Vi, I'm sorry. I would really have to wonder how a 9-5 office job would work out for me."

"You're a college grad, you'll do fine. You had to study for tests and for theory, and even if a lot of what you do is physical and social," said Astra, "there's a mind present. You wouldn't be so entertaining if you didn't."

"The good news is you'll be in and out of the office much of the time, carrying papers, delivering petitions, talking to people, traveling to the court house or various departments as a messenger. And you are going to need to replace a lot of what your room mates sold off, anyways," Vi said. "Well, not men's clothes," she smirked, patting his ass.

Vi added "It would be part time anyways, you can't do everything the job requires and others at work will have to pick up the slack until a qualified infill can be found. You may even have time to audition for roles, but no promises."

"Most workplaces just need someone who fits in," said Astra. "You'll be splendid and Vi can vouch for you. Most job candidates would jump at the chance for an internal recommendation and you'll get it in spades. Vi, I can write a letter as well if you need it, I have some pull because of my family; we're well known in labour circles even if my dad has to play a balancing act, politically."

Mymo nodded his head.

Vi gave a deadly, quiet whisper: "Don't fuck this up, cat boy."

She gently dropped Mymo to the floor. "Go, make your face," she said. "Nothing fancy, just believable. When you're done you can come back here and lie by my feet if you get bored and I'm still here, or you can go do your floor exercises and entertain Marci. Oh wait, speaking of Marci ..."

Mymo gave a tic of his head at the change in direction.

"She's going to approach you about a project. It would be good if you could help her – but be careful. Bring a pocketful of 'no, thank you Ma'ams' with you, she'll respect that and won't press."

The penny dropped on this morning's performance and Vi's "administrative action". Marci was a still waters run deep kind of person and, recognizing her weaknesses, helped prepare him to stand up for himself if he needed to. It was almost certainly a group effort.

"Why would you say that, Miss Vi?" he asked, squatting comfortable in the floor, legs bent and out, both arms straight down to the floor and touching between them.

Astra picked up the response. "She is, let me say, very creative in an out-of-the-box sort of way, and some of her ideas are really good at pushing boundaries. It's a part of why I love her so much," she added with a wistful smile.

Vi said: "When we were first talking about letting you stay, when it came to us trying to hide you from others, and before we realized you'd make a presentable woman, one of her suggestions was to hollow out a large stuffed bear and have you hide inside of it."

"In our room," said Astra. "But only until the coast was clear."

Mymo bit his lip again, slowly shaking his head until a thought occurred to him. "I dated a costume designer and would-be furry back in senior year. It was a couple years ago," he said. To Vi's sharply raised eyebrow he added on "we shared a class; we drifted apart when it was over but we're still friendly."

"She told me heat was always a problem with mascot costumes, especially when it's plush. There needs to be ventilation, a spotter, frequent breaks – and why the Hell am I even talking about this? It's like bondage, but with even more safety issues and training involved."

"Yeah, don't worry about it, just don't tell Marci," Vi said. "She'll go all engineer mode on that, and I'm not ready yet to have you sit around with a Steiff tag on your ear or a fluffy bear tail shoved up your -"

Astra coughed.

Vi blushed very slightly, and then said without skipping a beat "The inactivity would kill you and the heat's not good for your body. I'm an athlete, I know."

"But at least you've thought about it," Astra said, "so you'll be informed if she brings it up. And I do have to admit, it's really amazing to see you being so bloody open minded about all this weirdness, the cross-dressing, becoming a pet, and being so nonchalant about -"

Mymo interrupted with a wry grin and tone of voice. "Hey, I'm only collecting material for the talk show circuit for when I finally become famous, you know."

For this he was rewarded with a gentle kick from Vi.

Astra's eyes shifted. "Would you actually be open to this?" she asked.

"I've never really thought about that, not even when Carol bought it up in casual conversation." He paused for a moment. "I'm sure you and everyone else would have some fun with it but I'd have to think pretty hard on it."

"Well, no one present is asking you to," Vi said. Astra giggled but said nothing. "Although if it's light enough, I would seriously enjoy carrying you around, having my hand raise your paw to say hi, posing for pictures, taking you dancing or even skating on New Year's Eve ..." Vi stopped for a moment, vicariously enjoying the mental image which raised a more-then-slight blush. She shook it off.

"Anyways, you better scoot off like I said before dear, Women are at work now."

"Yes, Miss Vi, and thank you, Miss Astra," he said with a nervous smile, standing up and walking back into the hallway.

As he retreated, he heard Astra deeply chuckling, saying "Vi, you blushed! Twice!!" followed by "I did not! Well maybe just that once at the end." Astra's response was loud enough for Mymo to easily pick out: "Well then, which end then, hmmm?"

He shook his head and practically dove into the comfort room in his haste to get away.

Finis.

There will be more, look for future stories with the name 'Mymo' in the title.

NANA'S GAME

By Magda Fairelander

Carlos absolutely loved his grandmother. But going to her house after school was a chore - an increasingly unpleasant one. For one, Grandma was what the cable shows would call a hoarder. Teetering stacks of paper, magazines, mail, boxes of knickknacks. One would think that so much stuff would be an endless treasure hunt for a boy, but Grandma got surly about 'disturbing my things' and he ended up getting such an earful from his mom that exploration wasn't worth the effort..

Also, Grandma was old and ailing, more likely to spend her afternoons dozing in front of the ancient TV set than ... well, doing anything else. Even when she was more active, she was never the doting grandmother of stories, with pet names and fresh-baked goods, likely to slip candy or money into Carlos' pockets under his parents' noses. But the older he got, the more remote she became, settled in the large recliner in her living room, with little to say beyond, "Hi, honey" and "'bye, baby" when he came over.

At the age of ten - he didn't remember ever seeing Grandma outside of her house. On the front or back steps, at most, but never even past the fenced-in yard. It seemed weird but he never questioned it. It seemed like a thing that an old person might do. Even though his paternal grandmother -- who insisted on being called 'Abuelita' -- was old but still active, his friends talked about doing things with their grandparents: shopping, camping, crafts.

But Grandma never left her house, didn't cook much, always slept, That was just how she was, until Carlos found the chest. He discovered the chest under a pile of shoes in the back of his grandmother's closet. It was small, plastic encrusted with yellow paint and paste gems, like a cheap toy lacking a brand name. Only it had a real metal lock, and was surprisingly sturdy. He couldn't bust it open - not that he would, of course.

He had forgotten why he was in Grandma's closet in the first place. He wasn't supposed to be rooting around in her rooms but he finished his homework early and forgot to bring his portable game system with him and he was just ... so very bored. So he went into her bedroom and the closet door was ajar. The shoes piled on top of the chest were old and moldering, with stiletto heels he could scarcely imagine Grandma, with her sclerotic veins and swollen ankles, strapping to her feet.

A toy chest with a real lock confused him to the point where it stayed with him, irritating a tiny portion of his brain. Finally, his curiosity pushed him to search for a key. So over the course of several weeks, he searched for any stray key in Grandma's house, methodically tested each key he found in the chest lock he found in the house, until he was bored and wishing he had never found the chest..

What good was a chest without a key? He even asked his grandmother that night, before his mother came to take him home. She didn't remember where the key was or what was in the chest. Then again, she was starting to remember less each passing week. Did he waste a few afternoons on this pursuit? It felt that way. But he neither put the chest back nor forgot about its existence. And on yet another rainy afternoon, stuck inside without electronics, books or even home to distract him, he searched again for a key. And he found one, under a stack of papers that looked untouched in years.

Lock found. Key fitted. Dinky little chest opened. The inside of the chest was lined with black shiny fabric. There was something that filled the chest, wrapped in black velvet. Carlos unfolded the velvet and found a heart. That is, someone's heart.

He recognized it as an actual organ from a poster of the human body that was in his science class. It was not desiccated or withered. The flesh was pink and white, smeared with blood that should have dried long ago. That thought crossed his mind that this was some sort of movie prop for some long-ago horror movie. Grandmama had known weird people, back in her day -- Mom always said so.

Carlos reached out to feel the "blood," but when he placed his fingers on the heart, it beat ... once. A jerking, shuddering spasm expelled a spray of blood. He backed away in shock and fright, but managed not to scream. Then he edged close. Definitely a prop. For a movie, or a haunted house. It was an effect. There must be something under the heart, a mechanism sensitive to pressure.

Lifting the velvet out of the chest, he looked at the bottom of the container; it held nothing else. He rolled the heart over in the fabric, turning it over. No wires, no gears, no foreign parts. Breathing a little prayer to no one and nothing in particular that he wouldn't break this thing, he held the heart in his left hand and probed it gently. When it touched his bare skin, it began to beat again. Slowly at first, then increasing in strength, like a regular heartbeat. Because it was devoid of blood, the squeezing of the chambers and aorta were exaggerated. It flattened and expanded like a heavy glove.

Fascinated, Carlos slipped his fingers up the aortic valve, trying to feel for wires, strings, a battery. But there was nothing. It felt like meat, but it was still beating, squeezing his fingers as he poked into one of the lower chambers. Withdrawing his fingers, they were smeared with blood, so fresh that then he lifted his fingers to his face, he could smell the iron.

It was time to wake Grandma.

Carrying the heart in one hand and the chest in the other, Carlos ran downstairs to the living room, where his grandmother was dozing in front of the television. He made sure to yell in her good ear. "Grandma! I found this in your closet!"

Her heavily-cataracted eye was on the same side as her good ear, so her face was full of confusion until she turned her head to face Carlos. "Baby, what is it?"

Carlos frowned at being called 'baby,' but he asked, "Grandma, how does this work?" He thrust the heart in her face.

She inhaled sharply and sat up with more speed and agility than Carlos had ever seen from her before, snatching the heart and its box from his hands. "Boy, where did you find this?" She placed the heart back on the velvet but it continued beating.

"It was in your closet. Who made it?"

He had been staring at the heart, but when he looked into his grandmother's eyes, they were clear and piercing, the emerald coloring unclouded. His vision shifted, and when he looked at the heart again, it was obviously a real, anatomical heart, covered with blood. The chest holding it was black marble, inlaid with gold and precious gems.

"Grandma, how is that real? Whose heart is that? What was --"

His grandmother spoke again, and her voice was without quaver or breathlessness, full of steel and ice. "Sssshh. I cannot answer all of your questions. The years have not been kind, and there is not enough time.

"I don't remember whose heart this is. A wizard's, perhaps? Maybe a god? There were so many hearts. I thought I left them all behind ..."

Carlos stared down at his bloody hands, waiting to either wake up, start screaming, or both. But neither happened.

A rich, husky chuckle came from his grandmother. "You are made of sterner stuff than you know, boy. I hope it's enough to preserve you when the owner of this heart comes to retrieve it."

The boy whispered, "Was ... Is he a bad guy?"

Grandma sighed. "Again, I don't remember. What I do recall is that -- back then, I would not have cared."

He was silent, mouth hanging open.

"You are never to tell your mother how you found out. She has willed herself to forget much, which has made me forget ... would you like to see a glamor? This is tiring me, but I want to show you something."

Carlos fidgeted, biting his lip. "What's a glamour?"

"A glamour, my boy, is an illusion. Watch me."

She lifted herself out of the chair slowly, but when she stood, the woman was no longer Carlos' aged, fading grandmother. She was taller now, much slimmer and curvaceous. Long raven tresses framed her heart-shaped face, making her porcelain skin and Cupid's bow of a mouth all the more noticeable. A tiara of blood-red rubies crowned her, matching the deep crimson of the silk and lace gown that now clothed her.

This being took several steps towards Carlos, her heels clicking on the parquet floor. He backed away, which brought a cruel smile to her lips.

"Did no one ever teach you to bow to a queen?"

He fell to his knees, closing his eyes and wishing this was just a dream. Then he heard a snore. Opening his eyes and raising his head, he saw his grandmother, as he knew her, lying in her favorite recliner, once again asleep. On her stomach was the chest, looking as chintzy and unglamorous as before he brought it to his grandmother.

Moving quietly, so as not to wake her, he took the box and returned it to the depths of her closet. After that, he washed his hands thoroughly, put on a clean shirt and threw away the blood-stained one. He went back downstairs and watched TV. His grandmother did not stir until his mother came to pick up Carlos.

On his way out, his grandmother gave him a big hug and looked at him with just her good eye. "I love you so much, baby. Just as much as

I love your mom." She held his hands in hers, squeezing them as she kissed his cheek. "See you next week."

In the car, he opened his fist while his mother was distracted with rush hour traffic. In his palm was a key.

Of course, now that he had a reason to go to Grandma's, Carlos found all sorts of impediments in his path. His cousins had begged their parents to let him come over after school, who then begged his parents; his 5th grade teacher recommended him for a couple of after-school clubs he would have been excited about a few weeks ago; somehow, his dad prevailed upon his mom, Carlos's abuela, to babysit him a couple of times a week. It ended up being close to a month before he could go back and visit Grandma.

Okay, rifle through her stuff for more mysteries. He kept the key in his school bag - he had traced its outline, researched online what it would open, and sometimes, he just held it in his fist, until it grew hot and left an imprint on his palm.

When he was finally back at Grandma's house, he gave her a quick kiss and started searching immediately. He knew that the key would mostly likely fit a music or jewelry box. He had seen a few of those but remembering precisely where was an issue. After several false starts, he opened a linen closet upstairs near his mom's old bedroom and found the box that would unlock with his key. Sitting down within the closet, door left open for light, he opened the plain box, made of a hard, dark wood. Inside was a velvet bag, with something hard and semi-spherical inside.

Carlos poured the object out of the bag into an outstretched palm. Round on top but flat on the bottom, it was smooth-looking black gem, with a deep red cross on top, the redness highlighting the matte blackness of the stone. He shifted it gently in his hand, admiring how the light struck it but without any shine - the gem seemed to absorb any light that hit it, rather than reflect it.

Suddenly, the gem jumped out of his hand, its legs unfurling before it hit the floor.

He tried to back away but found that he couldn't move. Had it bit him? He didn't feel any pain. Confusion and panic, but no pain. He could not even call out his distress - he could only pant in a desperate rasp as the black widow crawled around him. It spoke in a crackly whisper: "Where is my queen?"

Carlos tried to take a deep breath but it felt like his lungs were unable to expand enough. His panic turned into terror, and he could only groan, "Downstairs."

It crawled onto his pant leg and sat on his knee. "That wretched hulk below?" It flexed several of its legs. "Why, it is she. What has this pitiful world done to her? Nothing she didn't deserve, to be sure." A strange sound, like paper being crinkled, came from it and Carlos realized it was laughter.

The pressure within his lungs eased, enough that he could breathe and whisper, "You know her well?"

More eerie, harsh laughter. "We wielded magic side by side for ages until she deserted me. Betrayed me. Leading me to this world with so little to feed on. I am starving for magic." It crawled up the boy's thigh.

Carlos tried not to stutter. "Were you ... her familiar?"

"Familiar? Ignorant boy! Familiars scrape and bow and fetch and simper. I was her catalyst! I fed off her magic and weaved spells for her use. We created so much beautiful magic together - no one stood in our way! She was magnificent and awful. Until she gave it up and had to flee for her life ... and she tried to LEAVE ME!" The little body shook with vehement rage.

He whispered, "Why did she give it up?"

The crackly voice sneered. "For love!" Another ugly laugh came from the creature.

Carlos felt it jump onto his bare arm and thought he was going to pass out from fear. He could taste acrid fluids rising to his throat, his stomach churning. He could feel each leg pressing against his skin and if he hadn't been paralyzed, he would have shook violently from head to toe.

"You. You're a product of her. Of her love." Never had the term love sounded so grotesque to him before. "I can practically taste her magic in you. You could feed me -- well enough to restore my power to return home. After I finish her off. It would be a blessing for her, poor thing - living in this world has ruined her."

It began spinning a web that wrapped around Carlos's arm, sticking to his skin. Carlos started to feel weak - too weak to fight, too weak to cry out or even beg. Rather than a dull grey, the web was shiny and black, with a glow that somehow hurt his eyes to look at. All he wanted was to sleep, but in a small part of his brain, he thought, "Grandma ... Mom ..."

A bright white light and a searing pain hitting his now-bare arm woke him up. He could breathe freely but was too scared to move. The bright light concentrated to a sphere held between his grandmother's hands, with a dark spot in the middle. Looking around him ... it wasn't near him. Did Grandma capture it in the sphere? He heard the crackly voice, muffled and diminished to a mere whisper. "My queen! Have mercy!"

Grandma had the glamor on again, looking restored to youth and power. "Ariadne, you served me well for so long. So you know ... I have no mercy."

Its final scream was felt more than heard but made Carlos's head ring. The white sphere winked out of existence, taking the dark thing with it and the familiar form of his grandmother stood over him. "Baby, are you alright? Did she hurt you?" Grandma hauled him up to his feet and spun him around, looking for wounds.

To his mortification, Carlos burst into tears and threw himself into her arms. With a strength he didn't know she had, Grandma picked him up and carried him downstairs, getting into her recliner and letting him cry himself to sleep. He awoke to his mother shaking his shoulder. "Are you okay? What happened?"

Grandma replied, "He was tired after doing his homework and took a nap, but had a nightmare. But he's okay now, right, baby?" His grandmother smiled at him and Carlos felt his heart lurch.

"Yeah, I just had a bad dream. Let me get my bag and I'll be ready to go, Mom. Love you, Grandma."

Later that night when alone in his bedroom, Carlos pulled out a small leather notebook that Grandma placed his bag without him noticing. Soft and worn, with semi-translucent leaves of something older than mere paper, Carlos scanned over the figures in the book, looking like the Egyptian hieroglyphics his class studied a while ago. A tiny, neat scrawl in English was written on the outer margin of the first page: "Keep safe, no matter what."

Carlos grabbed tracing paper and a pencil on his desk, turned the page, and traced the rune at the top right, then attempted to draw it freestyle, over and over until his head bobbed and his eyes fluttered shut several times. When he crawled reluctantly into bed, he tried very hard not to dream about anything that happened that day.

Weeks flew by for Carlos without seeing Grandma. He asked his mother about her and she replied that his grandmother had a cold and needed time to recover without a rambunctious boy tearing all over her house. Carlos took the explanation in stride and continued working on the runes. He couldn't find a translation, but his imitation of the writing progressed from painstaking tracing to freehand drawing to actually breaking out a calligraphy set he found in the attic and writing the runes in ink. He had no idea exactly what they meant, but with each practice, they felt more familiar, more a part of him.

Things seemed pretty ordinary, but every once in a while, he caught his mother looking at him with concern but she would turn away quickly when she saw him looking back at her. After the incident with Ariadne, he nursed his arm for a bit but otherwise - he thought everything was okay. But after a while, he started to get impatient to see his grandma again. He had so many questions, it was hard to concentrate on school or chores or playing basketball. Finally, after pestering his mother, she allowed him to go to Grandma's after school one afternoon.

"She's not well – in fact, we may need to put her in a nursing home soon. So be good, be quiet and do what she tells you to without any fuss."

"Yes, Mom."

But when he arrived at Grandma's house, she was more active than he had ever seen her before. Some of the towering piles were gone from the living room, the room had been dusted and Grandma was wearing something besides a housedress and slippers. She was standing up and holding a deck of cards when he came through the door.

"Grandma, are you alright," he asked?

"Child, we don't have time for questions. We have work to do."

"Work?"

Grandma smiled - an incongruously bright smile that didn't seem to belong on her aged, tired face.

"Well, work ... but also a game. Are you good at cards?"

He nodded slowly, confused by the change in her.

"I'm going to teach you a game. But first – have you been reading the notebook?"

"Er, yes, although … well, I can't understand what it says. But I've been drawing the figures and -"

"Show me."

He dropped his bag to dig out the notebook but she stopped him with a touch on his shoulder. "No paper. No pen. Show me like this."

She drew a rune in the empty air, only a soft fizzy light followed the the movement of her finger, lingering just long enough to make it appear whole before disappearing.

Carlos's jaw dropped and Grandma smirked.

"You try now. Concentrate. And believe."

He closed his eyes and called to mind one of the early runes he had traced over and over. Opening his eyes, he traced the air and a brief sputtering light that winked out before he could finish. But that he did it at all made him want to shout.

"Yeeeesssssss. I knew you could, baby. Keep practicing that way, and the book will start to make sense to you. But now, let me teach you that card game." She reached for his hand and eagerly pulled him into the kitchen.

"But, Grandma, Mom said you were ill -"

"Ssssh. It comes and goes. Today, it's gone. Tomorrow, I may feel worse. Which is why we need to do this today. You understand?" She sat down at the kitchen table and put down a deck of Tarot cards.

Carlos tried to keep a look of skepticism off his face but could tell by his grandmother's expression that he failed badly. "Those cards look like they're not for games."

"They are both for play and for serious things. She separated the deck into two, then shuffled each group. "Ever play a game of cards where the one who puts down the highest matching card wins the round?"

"Like War?"

"Something like that. But something extra. Pay attention. From this deck," she pointed to the taller stack of cards, "I'll deal us 7 cards. And from the other deck, we each get 3 cards. We'll take turns putting the first card down, and the other person has to beat that card by putting down a higher card. Whoever puts down the highest card wins the round ... but to claim the cards, they then have to put down one of the special cards as a trump. But the other player can then steal the round by putting down a higher trump card - the trump cards are numbered separately from the other cards. Does this make sense to you?"

He was chewing on his lip by this point, but nodded anyway. "Yes, I think so."

"Let's try and see."

The first part of the first round went quickly, with Grandma winning and laying down The Hierophant card. Carlos looked dubiously at his three Major Arcana.

"You can let me win or you can take the round from me with a higher card. Which is it, boy?" Grandma's voice was stronger and deeper than usual.

Carlos laid down the Strength card.

"Very good! You win!" Grandma pushed the cards towards his side of the table.

"Don't you get another shot with a higher trump card?"

"Nooooo. Just one trump card per round, and they don't go back in the deck. In fact, the goal of the game isn't to win the most of the regular cards - it's to take as many of trump cards as you can before they run out."

The boy frowned but pulled the cards towards him, putting each set in neat stacks.

In the second round, Grandma said, "Let's make this a little more interesting to watch, yes?"

She drew a rune in the air and the cards stood up on their own. The minor cards rocked and shuffled along, but the trump cards danced and spun, as if commanded to do a jig.

Carlos gawked, wide-eyed. "Could you always do things like this?"

"No ... I had to be trained. Magic is a skill, just like any other - but it helps to also have a talent for it." She pointed and one of her cards spun to the center. Once again, she won the round and sent The Judgment card dancing atop the other cards in the round. "What have you to counter?"

He started to pick up the card he wanted, but drew back his hand and pointed while thinking of the one he'd chosen. The Fool danced over to the center and leaped onto the Judgment card, knocking it over and taking its place on the top of the small pile.

"The Fool is the lowest number card, but like the Joker, it can also take on the highest value. Very good. But you weren't sure that would work, were you?"

"No, ma'am." Carlos blushed.

Several more rounds passed. Grandma won once. Carlos wondered if he was lucky or if Grandma was throwing the game to him. On his next draw from the Major Arcana pile, he ended up with the Death card. Any desire to play or to humor his grandmother fled and he felt sick to his stomach.

"You have my blood. My curiosity. My courage. You are worthy of my gift."

He looked up from the spinning, dancing cards in front of him to see her face, somehow blended - the old woman he knew and the young woman she was long ago. "What do you want to give me, Grandma?"

"My power, child. It won't be much – not nearly as much as I once had. But it will be enough for this world. You will have the power to do many things."

As Carlos chewed on that thought, the idea of power and what he could do, Grandma won the next round and presented her trump card: The Emperor. She drew a rune in the air. "This could be your future."

He felt bigger. Standing up, he walked to the living room where there was a full length mirror in one corner of the room. Now taller than his father, an adult face with his dad's nose and jaw and his mom's eyes stared back at him. Carlos rushed back into the kitchen. "Is this me or is it glamour?"

"It is both. It is how you may look one day. A man of influence and consequence. A man who would not be ignored by anyone. Do you counter my trump?" Carlos could feel himself recede back into his regular body. He shook his head and sat back down as Grandma grabbed her winning hand and put the cards in her corner.

"Child - if you are going to play a game, always play to win. Life will give you enough opportunities to lose without you forfeiting."

"What if I don't like the game, Grandma?"

"Sometimes, we don't have a choice - we must play the games life sets in front of us."

The Death card taunted him with its little dance. It wasn't fair that he had to play this game, that his Grandma was only now revealing her true self to him, that he was being forced to make a choice when there was so much more he wanted to know. The stakes seemed too high for a silly little card game.

He drew a rune in the air and the cards fell down onto the table, lifeless once more.

"I love you, Grandma but ... what if I don't want to be like you?"

"Old and tired and trapped in molder and decay? You won't, if you take this power from me."

"No! I don't want to be cruel and icy and willing to destroy people – that's who you were, wasn't it? I love you more as you are now, Grandma. I don't want your power, I want YOU ... please don't turn me into someone like you were."

Carlos bounced out of the chair and ran to his grandmother, threw his arms around her neck and hugged her tight as he sobbed. Seconds ticked by as he waited to be scolded, worse, punished for his outburst. Instead, her arms wrapped around him and she crooned softly in his ear, the sweetest sounds he had ever heard from her.

"So like your mother, Carlos. You have her heart. Even before she was born, I knew her love was more powerful than my magic. I had to protect that, protect her. I gave up all I knew so that she would be safe - from my enemies and from me. She is precious to me. As are you - I love you so much."

She stopped hugging him but held him by the shoulders. "I'm not angry, baby, but my time is nearing its end. No matter what, I will watch over you - your future will not be easy but you can persevere.

You are filled with love and you can do good in the world - with or without my magic. Stay true to yourself and don't be afraid to love."

Any other time, Carlos would have squirmed and blushed and tried to block out such words, but now, he nodded solemnly. "I promise, Grandma."

She yawned. "If you will put the cards away - I am going to go take a nap." She got up and shuffled out of the kitchen to her bedroom.

He collected the cards, then spread his schoolbooks out on the table to do his homework. When he went to check on her an hour later, she wouldn't wake up.

The night before his Grandma's funeral, Carlos eavesdropped on his parents talking in their bedroom.

"Is there a point in contesting the will?" his dad asked.

"I don't think so. Mama's attorney drew up a solid will. It's clear, she was of sound mind, there is nothing unreasonable." Mom replied.

"But why would she leave her house, and everything in it, to the boy? He's only ten - the house is nice, but what is he going to do with all of that junk? And what's with the provision that only he can say what can be thrown out?"

"The house is in a trust until he's 18, and she left enough money to cover taxes and the like far past when he'll come of age. Plus, we're trustees."

"But still - an entire house and everything in it - to a boy."

"Our boy."

"Should we move in? Rent it out? Can we sell it to pay for his college?"

"We can't, not until he comes of age. But according to the letter Mama left with the lawyer, we should give him the key and let him visit. He can take possession of any personal items whenever he wants."

His father sighed. "This may spoil him. Carlos is a good boy now, but this may go to his head."

There was a pause before his mother answered. "She thought the world of him. And how can I deny him her gift?"

At the cemetery the next day, Carlos kept his head bowed, hardly saying a word. Family, friends and acquaintances streamed by the casket, hugging and clasping hands with his mom and dad, pausing to pat his shoulder or pull him close for an awkward hug.

When only the 3 of them were left at the graveside, Carlos asked, "Can I have a little alone time to say goodbye? Pleeeeeaaaassssseeee? I won't be long, promise. I know you need to say goodbye, too, Mom."

His Mom, still red-eyed nodded and walked toward the car that brought them there, holding her husband's hand.

Carlos looked around to see whether anyone was watching, then knelt on the grass next to the casket. He closed his eyes, then drew a rune in the air, the one that called to him the most. Sparks lingered in the air from the movement of his finger.

A large black bird circled over the grave, then alighted next to him.

Carlos opened his eyes and went a bit pale. "Will you watch over her?" said the boy.

"There is no need to watch over her. I'm here to watch over you. You asked for protection," the bird replied. Carlos took a deep breath. A talking bird was less scary than a heart that beat without a body, or a magical spider. On the other hand ...

"Do I need protection? Am I in danger?"

"No. Or, at least, not yet. I don't know the future. I'm just here to protect you." The bird shivered and cawed.

Carlos whispered, "Thank you, Grandma."

The raven softly replied, "You're welcome, baby."

~ THE DARK ~

LUST

By Janeel Kharg

It was dark as Liz walked down the narrow street that night, the only faint light coming from a crescent moon and the myriad of twinkling stars whose light had travelled across countless aeons. In this out of the way place, street lights seem to have been considered unnecessary, a luxury. She pulled her scarf tighter around her neck, as winter was fast approaching and the air had a distinct chill to it.

There were few people around at this hour and the sound of her own footsteps sounded sharp and clear on the pavement as she hurried homeward. Liz wouldn't normally be out so late in a strange area, totally unknown to her, but her car had decided that this was a good day to die, and she couldn't call a cab as the battery on her mobile phone had also given up. If she'd seen a pay phone that was actually working you can bet she'd have used it to get help, but no such luck. Isn't that always the way? she thought.

She wasn't afraid; being out alone had never worried her but it was late, and cold, and she just wanted to get home. So when she sensed someone behind her it didn't worry her unduly; actually, she hoped it might be an offer of help, a lift perhaps, the use of a phone, something like that.

As the footsteps drew level she half turned to see who it might be and was quite taken aback. A young man, or apparently so, long hair, but dressed very snazzily all in black. Pale yes, but not your usual goth, no, much more dramatic, bohemian one might say. A wide brimmed hat, tilted over one eye, and a cloak of all things! Who wears a cloak in this day and age? she mused. An actor perhaps? On his way home from the theater? An artist possibly. A poser or eccentric? And is there a difference? Liz chuckled to herself at the thought.

Whoever he was, he was looking at her, quite obviously interested. Liz was unsure whether or not to speak and so just gave a small smile, friendly but not overly so. Easy does it, she told herself, don't go overboard.

"Ma'am," he intoned, raising his hat with a flourish and bowing low.

Ohhh that voice! Did she detect a slight trace of an accent? European, perhaps. And the tone was low, husky, warm. She shivered, briefly.

"Um, hello," she replied, feeling somewhat tongue-tied. Awkwardness was radiating from her in waves. She was not usually shy but this man was different from the usual pathetic creatures she tended to meet. Romantic without a doubt. And lord knows, she admitted to herself, I'm a sucker for romantics.

"Can I help you in some way?" she went on, hoping against hope that he would say yes.

His face lit up as a lazy smile spread across it, making his eyes crinkle at the corners, and a humorous twinkle positively shone out of them.

Liz's knees were now feeling quite weak. Yes, no prizes for guessing. She wanted this man. Oh, how she wanted him.

"It is late for you to be out alone, ma'am. May I walk you to your home or wherever you are going? Just to keep away unwanted attention. No strings,"
he assured her, smiling again.

"Why!" she positively simpered, "Yes, you may!"

It was still a good distance to her home and she was unusually impatient. Not prepared to wait so long, her desire rising by the minute, she halted at the first hotel they came to and, beckoning with her head, invited him to enter with her.

His eyes were now smouldering with desire. She could feel the heat of his body and smell his masculine odour and her mouth was becoming dry as her breathing deepened.

She booked a room from the bored looking desk clerk, took the key he proffered and almost ran up the stairs to the room on the floor above. Taking the key from her hand, her handsome would-be defender opened the door.

Trembling now with anticipation, and licking her dry thirsting lips, Liz entered behind him and looked briefly around the room. It was simply furnished, but clean. A bed, a dressing table. a small en suite bathroom. Good.

The two stood for a few moments just looking at each other, taking in every detail, then moved closer, mouths meeting, hot, hungry. Breath coming harder now, desire taking over entirely.

After a short time Liz pulled herself away from his lips and ran her hands lightly up his back, then entwined her fingers in his long hair and pulled gently but determinedly downwards until he sank to his knees. He gasped in anticipation, ragged breaths making his chest heave.

Wasting no more time, she bent down, pulled his head back, closed her eyes, and sank her teeth into his now prominent jugular vein....

A GOOD YEAR FOR THE ROSES

by Finn Fairelander

It's been a good year for the roses.

Once he was dead, she almost didn't want to bury him: but she had planned very thoroughly and was pleased with the way it had gone, although, of course, there were things she had not foreseen. The garden shovel, for example: she had planned on two strokes, the first to knock him out and the second to make sure, but she had been a little too enthusiastic. The shovel had stuck in his head, and she had had to struggle for a long few seconds to pull it free. Should she brace herself with one foot against his shoulder? She had laughed at the thought of the picture that would have presented to anyone passing by. Fortunately, the shovel had suddenly popped free with the strangest sound – a squelching noise brought short by a crack as the metal caught the edge of a piece of skull. Already he was much more interesting than he had been when alive.

The plan had always been to put him in the freezer at first while she dug the trench, and she was very proud of the makeshift pulley system that she had rigged up in the utility room to lift his body and gently push it into the icy chest. She had been emptying the freezer over the last two months to make room, for she did not want to waste any food by throwing it away, and even she could not stomach the thought of eating food that had been with him in the freezer. She lowered the lid and suddenly the house seemed light and empty and more cheerful than she could remember.

Next, she mopped up the blood – just about the amount of blood she had expected – and double bagged every scrap of newspaper and kitchen roll. She had made sure to buy those industrial strength garden rubbish bags, because although the bins were emptied first thing in the morning, she did not want to risk attracting flies until the bag had been safely dumped in the nearest landfill.

After trudging down the track with the rubbish, she filled the black bin at the side of a silent and empty road: back in the house, she mopped the floor thoroughly, tipped the dirty water down the drain with a bottle of bleach for good measure, and made a well-deserved cup of tea.

Over the next few days, she dug a deep trench in the back garden, right in the middle of his lawn. She didn't feel the need to go six feet down, but managed a decent depth, enough for his body and the rose bushes she had ordered from the garden centre. She knew that the ground would gradually settle over time as he decayed, but not too much surely and if it became noticeable, she would just have to think of something – maybe if she patiently laid down more layers of earth week by week that would do the trick. It would be interesting to see, she thought cheerfully.

When the time came to move him, she checked that her washing-line pulley was still knotted firmly to the loft ladder mechanism, and that the wheelbarrow was carefully placed right next to the freezer. She was expecting to get on with this briskly and efficiently, merely the next task in a long list of tasks, and was totally unprepared for the sight of his frozen body, every crease and hair delicately outlined in tiny frills of ice. For the first time ever she found him beautiful, and she hung over the freezer, blurring his outlines with her foggy breath. But after a while, she sternly told herself to make a start on this, the most physically demanding part of the process. She had to be careful: she wasn't sure that she actually believed that he would smash into thousands of little pieces if she was careless and let him drop, but she didn't want to find out. He lay awkwardly across the wheelbarrow, of course, and she carefully tied him to the handles: all she had to do was get him down two shallow steps outside the back door and then she was on the lawn, which was easy. The night was as still as she had ever known it, with a smudge of orange lights down in the valley the only sign of human habitation.

To her surprise, all she had to do was to tip the wheelbarrow gently and he fell neatly straight into the trench, almost as if he had climbed down and carefully laid himself down along the bottom.

She had been prepared for awkwardness, of having to spend time manoeuvring an unwieldy deadweight, but perhaps she was being unfair on his body, expecting it to be as useless and irritating as he had been in life. She felt no qualms at all as she tipped earth over him. She was merely getting the trench ready for the roses.

On the next morning she drove ten miles to the garden centre and picked up the five rose bushes, along with a bag of manure which the man said she should put in the bottom of the hole before planting the roses. She didn't say that she thought that the plants would have quite sufficient nutrients, and the thought of spreading a layer of manure on top of him amused her. She measured the depth of the trench with her eyes and again felt a ridiculous pride in her achievement – it was perfect, about two feet deep, so neat, and set right in the middle of the lawn. She couldn't wait to see the finished rose-bed, the first time he had ever given her flowers.

As spring turned into summer, she waited and imagined what was happening under her feet, as his body decomposed, skin splitting and changing colour, swelling then collapsing as its gases seeped effortlessly into the soil. Maggots and worms burrowed away and turned him into food for her roses, until all that was left were the rags of his clothes and his brown bones. Maybe one day these would be dug up, but not while this rose bed bloomed so magnificently. She was tempted to plant more, but as she said to herself, no other roses would look so good in comparison.

Unless she decided to get married again.

HONOR CODE

A Morality Tale by Raegan Summerisle

Part 1: Sin

Chapter 1: Violation

As the needle slid through her flesh and into her vein, Elizabeth unexpectedly found herself plagued by doubts and fears. Why was she doing this? Did she have to do this? Was this an absolute must?

She thought about her parents, her friends, her school, her future.

Could she have a baby?

She winced as the nurse probed with the needle for a moment, pausing as a small burst of red in the valve announced that the catheter was in place in the vein.

Elizabeth looked up at the nurse, her soulful brown eyes catching the nurse's attention. She finished taping the cannula in place on the teenager's arm and smiled gently. "Are you comfortable, Elizabeth?"

"No," admitted Elizabeth. "I'm a little scared. Is this going to hurt...?" She trailed off, not wanting to finish the sentence.

"Not at all, honey. A little discomfort, but mostly, you're not going to feel a thing."

I wasn't thinking about me, she thought. She blinked back tears. The nurse patted her arm. She wiggled on her back for a moment, trying to adjust her hips, feeling naked below, despite the sheet covering her, and her legs growing a little numb in the stirrups. She wiggled her toes.

The nurse hooked a line into her injection port. "Just saline, honey."

Footsteps out in the hall, and a moment later, a brief knock on the door. With barely a second's hesitation, the door swung in and the doctor entered, his nose buried in a chart clipped to a clipboard. He glanced up as he shut the door behind him.

"How're we doing?"

Terrible, thought Elizabeth, but she forced a smile. "Hi, Dr. Hall. I'm okay," she responded, without enthusiasm.

Doctor Hall patted her hand. "I know you're nervous, and I know you're having doubts, and I know you're upset, and I want you to know, that's all perfectly normal, Elizabeth. Let's get some medicine into you, and we'll get through this with you, and soon this will be just an unpleasant memory, okay?"

"Can...can I be asleep for this? Please?"

"Are you sure? Do you have a ride home?"

Elizabeth nodded. "Yes, Sir. I'm sure. And my roommate is here. She'll take me home."

Doctor Hall nodded. "In that case...Denise, if you would?"

The nurse slid a syringe into her IV and began to slowly depress the plunger.

"Elizabeth, you should feel really drowsy. You may not be all the way asleep, but you'll be very relaxed, and you can close your eyes, okay?"

Elizabeth nodded, her eyes half-lidded. "Thank you," she murmured.

The nurse and doctor watched her for a moment, then busied themselves around the table. The doctor arranged his instruments; the nurse adjusted a curtain over the patient's midsection. The monitor beeped steadily on the pole.

"She's ready, Doctor."

Doctor Hall flipped through the patient file. "She's 13 weeks in. We'll do a vacuum aspiration, then a quick dilation and curettage to make sure nothing is left behind."

Denise nodded. "Ready."

"Let's get moving, then."

The nurse removed the sheet that covered Elizabeth, exposing her, as the doctor slid over on a stool, snapping on a pair of latex gloves.

"Speculum."

Denise passed it over.

"Let's see now...okay...antiseptic, please."

"Here we are..."

"Thank you..."

"She's nicely dilated...this shouldn't be too bad..."

"Cannula, please."

Denise passed over the instrument.

"Thank you..."

Elizabeth groaned softly. Her slender body shifted a little.

Denise took her hand, squeezed it. "It's okay, sweetie, breathe, you're doing good."

"Suction..."

Denise passed the hose over and the doctor connected it to the cannula.

"Okay, vacuum on."

The machine hummed to life.

Elizabeth hissed softly, shifting on the table again, her eyes widening. "Cramps..." she groaned.

"You're okay, Elizabeth. Just keep breathing. Slow, deep breaths for me."

"You'll be finished in a moment, Elizabeth. You'll be ready to hit those books in just a little bit!" said Dr. Hall.

Denise sounded grotesquely cheerful. "That's right! What year are you?"

Elizabeth whimpered, a painful cramp rippling through her guts. "Fuh...first...year..."

"First year away from home, hmm?"

Elizabeth tenses, gritting her teeth. "Yessss...goddd...hurts..."

"You're doing good, honey."

"Forceps, please..."

"Here you go..."

"Just a bit of discomfort, Elizabeth...breathe..."

"Ooohhh...owww..."

"I know, honey...you're doing good. Try to breathe through it."

"Got it. You're doing well, almost there..."

Dr. Hall carefully manipulated the cannula. Elizabeth whimpered, her fingers gripping the sheets.

"Scope..."

Denise passed him the scope.

"Thank you..."

The doctor slid it in.

"A few...products...are still in there. Forceps..."

"Good...got it..."

"Now suction..."

"Got it..."

"I think we're about finished here."

The doctor stood up, slipping his gloves off.

Denise stroked Elizabeth's hand. "My niece goes to the local community college. Is that where you go, honey?"

Elizabeth shook her head groggily. "Nooo...I go...to...St. Catherine... of the...Holy Cross..."

Denise froze, and Hall stopped halfway to the sink, slowly turning back to Elizabeth.

"Are you...going home...after this?" asked Dr. Hall.

"I really think you need to go home a few days, maybe...?" added Denise.

"It would certainly be good, to lay down, rest, recover..." said Dr. Hall.

Elizabeth sighed. "I can't. I have an exam next week...I need to prepare for it."

The nurse looked up at Dr. Hall. He could read the concern in her eyes.

"Elizabeth...if I may suggest something before you rest up here a bit and finish with us today?"

Elizabeth shuddered. "Don't tell my parents?"

Dr. Hall shook his head. "No, not that, honey, but...just...don't tell anyone at your school."

The sun broke high over the lush green quad of St. Catherine of the Holy Cross University. Students and staff hurried along the tree-lined cobblestone walkways, between the dormitories and classroom buildings. The bells on the cathedral tolled the noon hour, the gong reverberating and echoing between the grand stone buildings of the busy campus.

Off the path, three girls lounged beneath the branches of a great oak, their excited chatter paused for the noon bells. Michelle grinned excitedly, eager to finish what she was saying, as the other two leaned forward with anticipation.

She finally burst out as silence returned, "I think I passed the test!"

The other two squealed happily, leaning forward to hug their friend.

"Congrats! You studied hard enough!" Christine smiled at her friend, genuinely happy for her success. The tall Asian girl, normally so very studious, possibly even a little cold, rarely broke her formal and stoic air. That she showed such emotion made Michelle and Megan even more happy. The black uniform of the prefect that Christine wore suited her serious disposition, most believed, rather than the blue uniforms that most students wore.

"You sure did study! No breaks at all! Not even to go for a coffee with me at the bakery!" Megan was the less serious of the three. Blond and sweet and clumsy, always thinking positively; perhaps a little dumb at times. Some upon meeting her might think her to be on the slow side. Her friends accepted the simple and naïve girl without care.

"Well, I had plenty of coffee in my dorm! And I did have one break. Poor Elizabeth, she was hurting for days!" said Michelle.

Megan pursed her lips. "That was last week. How is she doing? Still recovering?"

"She's fine now. The cramps are all over, she said, last night. No more bleeding. Goodness, I hope I never have to have anything like that done!"

Christine leaned forward, concerned. "What did she have done again? A cyst removed?"

"Yeah. Ovarian cysts, that they had to remove, she said."

"That's pretty awful," said Megan. "I think my aunt had something like that. Some sort of cyst...she couldn't have kids."

Michelle nodded. "It was awful. But she was in and out in record time. They were pretty fast, two hours, tops. I went and had breakfast and read."

"That is fast!" exclaimed Megan.

Christine frowned. "Was she in pain before the surgery?"

Michelle hesitated, thinking. "I...I don't think so? Not that she ever mentioned. She just asked me to take her to the women's clinic in Boyertown, that she was having trouble with cysts. But she never mentioned any pain? Why?"

"My dad's a doctor. An OB-GYN. He was talking about it with mom once, because she DID have issues with ovarian cysts. And they're actually pretty common, but it's not something they operate on, typically, because they usually go away on their own. I suppose they might operate, if the pain was bad enough? Mom had all kinds of issues. Constant tummy pain, pain when using the toilet, agony during her period, and more."

"That's horrible! I can't imagine! My goodness!"

Christine nodded. "You don't want to imagine, trust me. I saw enough, I hope it never comes to that! But we've known Elizabeth for most of this year, and she's never mentioned any of that. And I think she would have?"

Michelle shrugged. "You're right. I've known her for years. She would have told me, long ago."

"Which doctor did she see in Boyertown, anyway?"

"The one on 7th street. Boyertown Women's Health. The waiting room was kinda gross. Mostly pregnant women and brochures about..."

Michelle trailed off, frowning.

"You don't think?"

"Think what?" asked Megan, perplexed.

Christine frowned. "I hate to even imagine..."

Elizabeth yawned softly, her eyes heavy. She was sitting at her desk, slumped over her electronic reader, a History text slowly scrolling on its screen. She was about to turn it off when the door burst open and Michelle entered, a fistful of mail clutched in her hand. "Mail call!" she exclaimed.

"Oooh, anything good?"

"Credit card bill for me...remind me to send that home...junk mail...junk mail...more junk mail..."

"Something about my car's extended warranty? I don't even have a car!"

"Something for you, from your doctor." She handed Elizabeth the envelope.

"Thank you!"

Elizabeth leaned back in her chair, slitting it open with a pen, and slipped the papers out. She pursed her lips, scanning the info, then re-folded the papers and put them back in her desk drawer.

"Just a bill. They always get you those in time!"

Michelle laughed. "No kidding!" She looked at her roommate, concerned. "How're you feeling? All better?"

Elizabeth nodded. "Much better! I'm ready to go out on the town!"

Michelle grinned. "Woot! That is awesome! How'd you do on the test yesterday?"

Elizabeth grinned, held up her hand for a high five. "Another A! Thank God! He truly has blessed me here!"

Michelle cheered, slapped her roommates' hand. "You got that right! I feel like I have to fight for a C! I don't know how you do it!"

Elizabeth smirked playfully. "Studying! You never did get that part down right!"

The girls laughed, and Michelle hugged her tightly. "I'm so proud of you. Straight A's, even after surgery. Seriously, you're amazing. Want to go out tonight? Get a coffee, head over to the outlets, find a new outfit?"

Elizabeth smiled. "You're the best. And why not? Celebratory coffee is yummy coffee! I need a shower first, though. Staying here?"

Michelle nodded. "I'll wait. Close my eyes for a minute on your bed. Hurry up!"

Elizabeth stood up and stretched. "That sounds good." She picked up her bathroom bag. "I'll be back in 15 minutes!" She headed for the showers as Michelle stretched out on her bed. She closed her eyes, counting slowly to sixty, then opened her eyes and sat up, looking at the door. Her head slowly turned, eyes on the desk. She rose, opened the drawer, slid the mail out from the doctor, and read it. A hand lifted slowly to her mouth.

"Oh...oh, no..."

She folded the letter, slowly, and placed it back in the drawer. Then she fled the room.

Chapter 4: Intervention

Christine and Michelle walked slowly along the quad, alone.

"I sent her a text. Told her I had to run to the store, made up a lame excuse." Michelle sighed. "I...I'm terrified. I don't want her to get kicked out. I don't want to see her punished, either. She...she's not a bad person. She just...she did a bad thing..." She began to cry.

Christine hesitated, slid an arm around her friend, and hugged her. "I know. I just met her a few months ago, and I love her so much. Not just as a sister in Christ, but as a friend, a real friend, too. Every bit as much as I care for you. But..."

She sighed.

"What she did..."

"She made a mistake, Christine. A bad mistake. It...it could happen to any of us..."

Christine pushed her out, held her at arm's length, frowning. "Seriously? You know better than that! If you adhere to the code...to the teachings of the Bible and Church...no. No, it can't to us. The Code protects you, Michelle!"

"I know! I know all that! And I do adhere to the code!"

"Who was it, anyway?"

Michelle tilted her head quizzically. "Who was what?"

"Who was she seeing? She never mentioned a boyfriend, or anyone of interest to us?"

"Oh. She saw some guy from St. Sebastian a few times over the past few months. I guess it was him."

"When she saw him, did she go in a group? Did you go with her? You're her roommate and sister, after all," Christine pointed out.

"No...no she didn't..."

"So she went alone?"

Michelle nodded, eyes downcast. "Yes…"

"Did you know she was going on a date?"

Michelle shook her head. "Not the first time, no. She told me after. I knew when she went after, though. She never let me meet him, though. They always went off-campus somewhere."

"Oh, Michelle…" Christine squeezed her hand in hers. "All of that, and you didn't report her?"

Michelle looked shocked. "Report her? Christine, she's my best friend!"

Christine glared at her. "Michelle, when you came to this school, you signed the same thing that I signed last year when I came, and that I signed again this year as well. A pledge to adhere to the Honor Code. A pledge to be a Godly woman. A pledge to not smoke, to not use drugs. A pledge to only go on dates in groups, and to never be alone with a guy! Why do you think that Honor Code exists?"

Michelle whispered, "To avoid situations like this…"

Christine nodded. "You share in her sin, Michelle. You could have prevented this, had you reported her. As her friend, as her sister in Christ, it would have protected her from herself, from temptation, had you obeyed your pledge."

Michelle looked down at the ground between them. "I just didn't want to see her paddled or caned or grounded for the rest of the term!"

"So you would rather she be put in a position where she felt that having an abortion was the only choice she had?"

"I…I never thought…"

Christine nodded. "I know you didn't. But you have to be strong now, and file a report with the Honor Court."

Michelle whimpered. "I...I can't...I don't know that I can..."

Christine shook her lightly. "Michelle, I'm a prefect. If you don't do it, then I have to. I'm sworn to God, to follow the Honor Code, and I will do it. Not just for Elizabeth, but for you, and for myself should I commit a violation. I'm sorry. This would be better coming from you, and not from me. I'm sorry, sis, but it's because I love you both."

Michelle quickly shook her head. "No! I...I don't want to put you in that position. I guess I'll do it...I'll file a report immediately..."

"I'll pray for you. Both of you. I know it's hard, but you're doing the right thing."

Chapter 5: Denunciation

Elizabeth was lounging in bed, her electronic reader in hand, when her cellphone vibrated. She checked the incoming name and frowned, then answered it.

"Hello?"

The frown deepened.

"Yes, I should be? In half an hour?"

She paused, listening.

"Why is security coming here?"

She sat up.

"No, I don't understand? Take a report? Report for what?"

She stood up, shaking.

"Wait, what? If I'm not here when security gets here..."

Fear set in.

"What do you mean, kicked out of school? No!"

She slumped back onto her bed, fighting off tears.

"Of course, I'll be here!"

She slammed the phone down next to her and burst into tears as the dorm room opened. Michelle entered, nose buried in her phone, only to look up, startled, seeing Elizabeth on the bed, crying silently.

"Oh, you're in! I thought...I thought you'd be out at class, or...what's wrong?"

"I don't know! I don't know what's going on! That was the Campus Security Office!"

Michelle turned pale.

"Cam-campus Security? They called you?"

"Yes! They're coming here, said if I'm not here in half an hour, that I'd be promptly expelled!"

Michelle slowly sat, stammering, "Goodness! Is...were you caught... ummm...cheating, or something?"

"No! I don't cheat! But...I wonder...if someone saw me with Mark? We went out a few times, and...I don't know...maybe they turned us in? I never really paid much attention to who saw us or who knew...I know they don't like us dating..."

"Oh, Beth..."

Michelle burst into tears.

"I had to. I had to report you! We signed that Honor Code, and if I didn't, Christine would have! They know, Beth! They know about the abortion!"

"You told them? Michelle! You're my best friend, how could you!"

"I had to! We signed that pledge, Beth!"

"It's 2052, for God's sake. What I did was private, and it wasn't illegal! What are they going to do, pray for me?"

"Beth, did you read any of the Honor Code and Discipline material? Did you look at any of it? Didn't you see what happened last week, when they flogged Constance when she was caught smoking? She spent a day in the stocks on the quad!"

"But this was a private medical decision! The administration, the Dean, the Pastor, the stupid Honor Court, they have no business in this. Gosh darn you, Michelle..."

Michelle quoted, rolling her eyes, "'Veiled profanity is still profanity.' Honor Code, section 1. Don't make me report you again."

Elizabeth couldn't help herself. The anger broke and she giggled. After a moment, both girls were hugging each other and laughing.

Elizabeth finally broke free and pushed her friend away. "I'm still mad at you."

"I know. I don't blame you. But I'm mad at you, too. You put me in this predicament! So did Christine!"

"What's done is done. At least I know what I'm walking into. "

Elizabeth sighed.

"Everything will be alright. They'll probably cane you, ground you for the rest of the term. You should probably call Mark and tell him," said Michelle.

Elizabeth shook her head. "No, he's already dumped me. He dumped me before I even went to the doctor. I think he left his school, too."

"Oh, Beth...I'm sorry."

Elizabeth shrugged. "I shouldn't ever have let him touch me. I can't believe I let him touch me. One time...just one time..."

They both heard the footsteps in the hall and the pause outside their door. A moment later, a brisk knock echoed in the dorm room. Elizabeth sighed and opened it.

"Hi..."

The campus security guard entered, his black uniform nearly glowing under the room's lights. "Good afternoon, Miss. I'm Officer Wentworth. Which of you is Elizabeth Jones?"

Elizabeth reluctantly raised her hand. "That's me."

Officer Wentworth looked at her and nodded. "I need to see your school ID. Then I'm here to escort you to the Security Office. We need to take a full report on a recent activity that you were involved in."

Elizabeth dug into her purse and retrieved her identification. "Whatever. I'm ready, let's go."

The guard accepted and examined it, then handed it back. "You don't need to bring anything with you but your purse, Miss Jones. Let's go."

Chapter 6: Imputation

The lobby of the Security Office was empty when they arrived. Wentworth opened a door and stepped aside, allowing Elizabeth to enter the office area. He gestured to a chair next to a desk. "The detective will be with you shortly, Miss Jones. Please be seated."

Elizabeth rolled her eyes. "Detective? Seriously? There's no great mystery afoot!" She realized she was almost screaming.

Wentworth looked pained. "Miss Jones, please, be calm. I'm sure we'll clear all this up, okay? Just wait for the detective."

"Whatever!" Elizabeth slumped in the seat, starting angrily at the wall behind the Detective's desk.

The wait was only about ten minutes before the detective arrived. Elizabeth looked up to see another glistening black uniform, the man wearing it middle-aged and smiling pleasantly.

"Good morning, Elizabeth! I'm Detective Dennell, and I've been assigned to your case. Hopefully we can get this all straightened out, and get you on your way shortly, right? Right!"

Elizabeth couldn't help but return the smile when the detective answered his own question. "Hi," she responded.

The detective took out a clipboard and pen. "As you know, Elizabeth, this is an Honor Code investigation. Our office handles not just normal criminal activity here on the campus, but Honor Code violations as well. Now, I understand that there was an incident last week. It's my job to get a full report and to present it to the Honor Court."

"I didn't do anything wrong!"

"Elizabeth," said the detective, soothingly, laying down his pen and taking her hand between his. "It's not my decision to make, young lady. I'm only here to gather information, nothing more. Before we begin, I want to advise you on your rights as a student here at St. Catherine of the Holy Cross University. I need you to listen very carefully and to not interrupt me. Is that understood?

Elizabeth nodded, dejectedly. "Yes, Sir."

The detective squeezed her hand, reassuringly, and she smiled again, slightly, taking some measure of comfort from the kind officer. "Good girl. Now, you have the right to leave this University before any formal charges are made against you. If you choose to exercise that right, you will be sent home, and your parents or guardians made aware that you were expelled, not just for Honor Code violations, but also for the nature of the violations. Is that understood?

Elizabeth paled. "No...please, no. I don't want to leave this school. I love this school. I didn't do anything wrong!"

Detective Dennell nodded. "Hush and listen." He continued. "You have a right to not incriminate yourself. You don't have to talk to me or to anyone else. You may stand mute on any charges that are brought against you. If you choose to remain mute and to not participate in the ensuing investigation, you will be sent home, and your parents or guardians made aware that you were expelled for Honor Code violations. Is that understood?"

Elizabeth burst into tears. "I will stay! I'll stay! I didn't do anything wrong!"

The detective reached into his desk and brought out a box of tissue. He set it in front of Elizabeth. "Miss Jones," he said, softly, "please. Calm down. Let me finish, and you listen, closely, and carefully."

Elizabeth fought for control, gasping. She took several tissues and wiped her eyes. "I'm sorry!" she cried. "I'm sorry. I'm trying. I am." She hiccupped and caught her breath, forced herself to relax.

"Would you like some water?" Detective Dennell gestured to Officer Wentworth, who was standing passively by the door, observing. "Bring her some water, please, Daniel."

"Yes, Sir." He went to the water cooler and returned with a paper cup, setting it on the desk in front of Elizabeth, who took it gratefully and sipped.

"Thank you, Sir," she whispered.

Detective Dennell continued. "If you are found guilty of any Honor Code violations, or laws, you may be subject to Administrative Discipline. You have a right to refuse Administrative Discipline. Should you choose to refuse Administrative Discipline –

Elizabeth interrupted. "I know, I know! I'll be sent home and my parents told that I was a whore!"

The detective sighed. "Yes. You will be sent home, and your parents or guardians made aware that you were expelled for Honor Code violations. And I can see that you understand your rights." He passed a piece of paper and pen to Elizabeth. "Sign this." She did so, and Wentworth added his signature to a witness space.

"Miss Jones, I am troubled, and not by your supposed violation. You seem to be taking a very cavalier attitude to these proceedings. When you chose to come here, did you even bother to read the Honor Code, or to examine the Disciplinary Office's writ?"

Elizabeth shook her head slowly. "No, Sir. I...I skimmed it. I've never been in trouble, and I've never broken any laws that I know of. I go to church, I don't profane the Lord, or use drugs, or anything like that. I know this school uses corporal punishment, I've seen girls in the pillory, whipped, caned, whatever, but I...I believe I did nothing wrong. I do."

Detective Dennell nodded. "I see. Miss Jones, the Honor Code is more than the law. It's a Biblical Code of Conduct that you are expected to adhere to. Do you understand what that means?"

Elizabeth snapped back, "I'm not an idiot, Sir. Of course I understand!"

The detective nodded. "You've witnessed Administrative Discipline, as you noted. When an infraction is deemed severe enough, typically a public example is made. Most of the time, it's a day or two in the pillory on campus, as 'Penance,' and a public whipping or caning, for what they call 'Grace.' Sometimes less, sometimes more, it depends on the infraction. I really can't say what they would deem for you, as that's not my call. Personally, I'd send you home and let your parents deal with you. That's probably the least painful choice."

Elizabeth shuddered and shook her head. "My dad's an Elder in the Church...I don't think I'd consider the thrashing I got from him to be painless. And to tell him I was kicked out for an Honor Code violation...it would kill him. I can't. He and Mom both graduated from here. I need to finish." She sighed, slumped back in her seat, and sipped her water. "I understand my rights. I'll face the music. Whatever you do to me here has to be easier than what Daddy will do to me."

The detective nodded. "Sign this, please. Officer Wentworth, please sign as a witness that Miss Jones has waived her right to go home, and willingly accepts any judgment and any assigned disciplinary action."

Elizabeth signed her name and passed the pen to the other officer. "Done, Sir."

Officer Wentworth added his name. "Done, Sir."

Detective Dennell took the form and examined it, then added his own signature and slipped the paper into a folder. He settled back in his chair, his notebook in front of him and his pen in his hand, preparing to take notes.

"Clearly, Miss Jones, you know why you're here. Someone reported you for an Honor Code violation. At this time, I cannot give that name, but – "

Elizabeth interrupted. "It was my roommate, Michelle."

Inspector Dennell dipped his head in silent acknowledgment. "As I was saying, but in time, if you request a trial, you can face your accuser there."

Elizabeth shook her head. "That's fine. What do you need from me?"

Detective Dennell checked his notes. "Tell me what happened last Tuesday, September 18?"

"I had my roommate take me to Boyertown Women's Health Clinic. I had an appointment at 2pm."

"And what was the purpose of the visit?"

Elizabeth sighed. "My boyfriend...he...he and I...had an accident. I was pregnant. I went to the Clinic to end the pregnancy."

"And did you terminate the pregnancy?"

"Yes, Sir."

"How far along was the pregnancy?"

"What does that matter? Why does any of this matter? I had an abortion, I didn't break any laws!" cried Elizabeth.

"It matters, Miss Jones. Please answer the question. How far along was the pregnancy?"

Three months, okay? He was three months along."

"He? That answers my next question, then."

"I don't understand why it matters!"

Detective Dennell looked up. "Did the father know?"

Elizabeth nodded. "He knew. He tried to talk me out of it. He wanted to get married. I'm not ready, I don't really love him, it was just...just a one-time thing. He dumped me when I told him what I was going to do. Left his school, and I haven't heard from him since."

"And the father's name was Mark Johnson?"

Elizabeth looked shocked. "How do you know that? Yes, it was Mark Johnson."

"We put an inquiry in at St. Sebastian. He was the only student that recently left."

Elizabeth sighed. "What other information do you need?"

"What did you tell your roommate, who drove you? Did she know about the abortion?"

"No, Sir. She thought I was having some cysts removed."

The detective nodded and made a note. "Do you want a hearing? Or do you just want to accept the decision of the panel at the Honor Court, and the adjudicator at the Administrative Discipline Office?"

Elizabeth thought for a moment. "I'll do a hearing. I don't feel like I deserve punishment. I did nothing illegal. My body, my choice, and I believe in that."

Detective Dennell nodded. "Sit tight, then. We should hear back relatively shortly."

The courtroom was a formal meeting room in the Administration offices of the campus. A long table with three seats on one side, and several more seats opposite. A pitcher of water surrounded by several glasses was set in the center of the table. Detective Dennell guided Elizabeth into the room, followed by Officer Wentworth, who remained standing by the door. "Over here, Elizabeth," whispered Dennell. She wondered if he knew he was whispering. The two of them sat at the table and waited.

Their wait was only a few moments. The door opposite opened, and a uniformed officer entered. "All rise."

Elizabeth and the Detective obeyed, rising from their seats.

"The Honor Court is in session. The Honorable Justices, Judge Tracy Leverknight, Judge Mary Star, and Judge Richard Warner presiding."

The three judges entered, black robes swishing around them. Judge Leverknight, a tall thin older woman with a pinched face and greying hair, spoke briskly as she sat. "Thank you, Officer Middleton. Be seated."

Detective Dennell and Elizabeth sat. Officer Wentworth and the court officer remained standing, Wentworth at the door behind Elizabeth, and the court officer next to the door the judges had entered.

Judge Leverknight glanced through her notes, then settled a pair of startlingly icy blue eyes on Elizabeth. "Thank you for joining us today, Friday, February 28, 2052. A gathering of the Honor Court is a serious matter. Any time a student or faculty member stands accused of an Honor Code violation, we must take it seriously, and investigate the circumstances, and determine what Penance may be assigned, and, if necessary, what Grace is needed, not just for the salvation of the accused, but also as a lasting example for the flock, our student body."

She cleared her throat and looked at Elizabeth again. "Miss Jones, do you wish for an advocate on your behalf?"

Elizabeth shook her head. "No, Ma'am. Thank you, Ma'am."

"Then let's see what we have here."

Judge Star, a petite woman with dark red hair, leaned forward. "We have read the accusation. It seems that there is no doubt that Miss Jones is guilty of multiple Honor Code violations from Section 2. Dating outside of a group. Promiscuity outside of marriage. But what is most troubling is your cavalier attitude toward the worst of what you stand accused of – the abortion itself. How do you feel about what you did, Miss Jones?"

Elizabeth was stunned, her mouth dropping open in shock at the frankness. "Uhhh...Your Honor, I'm comfortable with saying that, I broke no law. Abortion is perfectly legal. I underwent a legitimate medical procedure that is perfectly legal in all 47 out of 65 states, and legal here. I fail to understand why I'm even in here." She leaned forward, looking from Judge to Judge. "Whatever happened to a hundred years of women's rights? I made a mistake. I went on a date. I had sex. I got pregnant, through no fault of my own. I had an abortion. I don't understand the big deal." She sat back, her hands clenching, her voice rising as her anger grew. "I'm a student of good standing here. My professors will all say as such! I get mostly A's. A baby would ruin my life! I'm too young to be a mom, I'm only 19 years old! I had no choice!"

Judge Warner cleaned his throat and stared coldly at her. "Miss Jones, have you no shame?"

"Shame? I don't know, a little? I wish I had a better opportunity? I wish I never gotten pregnant? But the abortion? No, Your Honor, I don't regret my decision. It was the right one."

Judge Warner leaned forward. "So you do not regret it? You would do it again? Please, Miss Jones, take but a moment to think before you answer my question."

Elizabeth paused for a moment before answering. "Yes...I guess I would. I believe in my body, my choice."

The judge shook his head. "Miss Jones, my body, my choice is all well and good if you're having your ears pierced or a necessary medical procedure performed. You made your choice when engaged in premarital sex. The idea of 'your body, your choice' ended there with the man you chose to copulate with. A fetus, Miss Jones, is not a part of your body. It's in your body, and you nourish it, yes – but that is a being, independent of you, with a unique destiny and a unique soul. You took that destiny away from him and sent his soul back to God. Do you understand that, Miss Jones?"

Elizabeth shook her head. "I'm sorry, I disagree. I'm too young to be a mother. I have a future, and right now, a baby is not a part of it."

Judge Star tapped the table. "Miss Jones, did you consider adoption?"

"No, Your Honor. I could never give my baby up."

Judge Star tilted her head. "But you could murder your baby?"

"That's not fair!" burst Elizabeth.

Judge Leverknight turned to the detective. "Detective Dennell, was Miss Jones this candid, this unconcerned, in your office, when you took your report?"

The detective hesitated before answering, then nodded. "Your Honor, it is entirely fair to say that Miss Jones does not grasp the seriousness of the situation. I think it is appropriate to add that she has only a fleeting understanding of the Honor Code that she signed, and no understanding of the Administrative Discipline to which she may be given.

Judge Warner asked, "Miss Jones was offered a chance to take expulsion?"

"Yes, Your Honor. She feels she committed no wrongdoing, as you heard for yourselves, and does not want her parents to know of her charges."

Elizabeth raised her hand. "And I still feel that way. I'll happily accept whatever punishment you deem necessary. Flog me, put me in the stocks. But I did not commit any illegal act. I did not violate the law. If you send me home, I will talk to an attorney about my rights."

Judge Star smiled thinly. "Miss Jones, your rights extend only so far as what you have agreed to when you signed your pledge when you enrolled. Your parents signed you into our care. You signed an acknowledgment to abide by the laws of St. Catherine of the Holy Cross and to the Holy Church, whose laws trump all Federal and State laws on Church-owned property. You swore to uphold our values, our laws, and to accept our Code of Conduct, the Honor Code, which you clearly did not take the time to read. You reiterated these vows with both Detective Dennell and Officer Wentworth as witnesses.

Elizabeth nodded. "I did, Your Honor."

Judge Warner tapped the table. "Have you any concern about what happens to you here? Or to your soul in the ever-after?"

Elizabeth blinked. "I...I'm not exactly a Christian, Your Honor. I don't really adhere to any faith. I believe in God, I suppose, but not... not how the Church portrays Him?"

Judge Warner was stunned into a momentary silence. The three judges stared at her.

"Then why, in the name of God, did you come to this University?"

"Because my father is an Elder in the Church, and my best friend, Michelle, who turned me in, I wanted to come here with her. And you have a good early education program. I want to be an elementary school teacher."

Judge Leverknight leaned forward. "Let me get this straight. You want to be around children, even as you engage in irresponsible pre-marital sex and terminate the life of an infant? Do I understand that correctly, Miss Jones?"

Elizabeth scowled. "I terminated a fetus. Not a baby."

Judge Warner stood up slowly. "Miss Jones...Elizabeth. I want you to see and hold something. He stepped around the table and approached Elizabeth, something in his hand. He took her hands in his, pressing an object into her palms. "Look at that, Miss Jones."

Elizabeth stared mutely into her hands. Tears threatened to well in her eyes.

"What you have there, young lady, is something I picked up from the science department on my way to today's hearing. It's a life-size model of a three month-old infant in the womb. Look at it, Elizabeth. Look closely. Ten fingers and ten toes, each developed, each hand strong enough to grasp. Arms and legs, a body, and a head. A developed central nervous system – it tried to escape the vacuum that was tearing it apart!"

The judge leaned forward, his finger touching the plastic model, as he spoke.

"Look at its face, Elizabeth. A face that never had the chance to look upon our world, to determine his own fate. A face that the doctor's forceps burst apart like a grape when he suctioned it out of your womb."

Elizabeth, shaking, pushed the plastic fetus back to the Judge. "Your Honor...I...I did what I had to do...I don't believe this...you will not shame me into remorse...I did the right thing, for my future! I had an abortion...I didn't...I didn't go and murder a baby! It's not the same thing!"

Judge Star interjected. "So, you didn't kill an infant? Just what do you think you might have given birth to, had you carried your son to term?"

Elizabeth cried out, "I did not! I did not kill a baby! I just...I had an abortion...a perfectly legal option I chose! And I'd do it again!"

Judge Leverknight shook his head. "I have heard enough. We are starting to go in circles. Judge Warner, Judge Star, have you any additional questions?"

Judge Warner shook his head, his eyes remorseful as he looked at Elizabeth. "No questions."

Judge Star shook her head. "I've heard enough."

Judge Warner nodded. "I'm ready to move forward." He returned to his seat.

Judge Leverknight looked at Elizabeth. "Miss Jones, do you have anything to say on your behalf that will inspire us to go gently on your case?"

"Your Honors, I'm a good student. I'm a good person. I made a bad choice, and I'm sorry, but I still feel I made the right decision for my life at this time. I don't know what to say. I don't want to be expelled, but if you feel that's the right thing to do, then I accept it. I pray you won't. I love this school. I love my classes, and my classmates. I want to continue my education here, but if I have to find a secular school, so be it."

Judge Leverknight nodded. "Thank you, Miss Jones. Officer Middleton?"

Officer Middleton straightened. "All rise."

Elizabeth and Dennell rose, followed by the three Judges, who filed out of the room.

Elizabeth looked at Detective Dennell. "Now what?"

"Now we go back to the Security Office and wait."

Chapter 8: Deliberation

The three judges retired to a comfortable room and removed their robes, then slipped into comfortable chairs around a small round table.

Judge Leverknight cleared her throat. "I think we can all agree on the guilt of the accused? We can move right to Penance and Grace?"

Judge Warner nodded. "Absolutely."

Judge Star agreed. "Yes."

Judge Leverknight sighed and rubbed her eye. "The child is not in a state of grace."

"Is it our responsibility to ensure her salvation?" asked Judge Star.

"Of course not, but it is our responsibility to give her every opportunity to make amends, to make herself right with God, and to achieve that salvation that is hers, by the sacrifice and blood of the Son," answered Judge Leverknight.

"The required Penance is not in doubt, then. How long shall it last?"

Judge Leverknight thought for a moment before she answered. "There is no prescribed length of time. But, for this? I feel an example needs to be made."

Judge Star tapped the desk with her pen. The others looked at her. "The infant was three months old. How about three days?"

Judge Leverknight scoffed. "She'll never do three days!"

Judge Star shrugged. "She might. We can feed and water her. And if she can't do three days, then she goes by the Grace of God."

Judge Warner nodded. "I like it. Three days of Penance feels right."

"Before we write this up, do you want to discuss, at all, any possibility of standard Administrative Discipline?" asked Judge Star.

Judge Leverknight looked up from her notes, startled. "Are you having doubts, Sister Star?"

Judge Star nodded, sadly. "She reminds me of my daughter. I know she isn't deserving of the usual punishment, but...we haven't had a case like this in years."

Judge Warner interjected. "We haven't had a case in ten years because the last example made, the students remembered, and passed the story down. They were still talking about it, up until about two years ago. Miss Jones could very well be saving souls by her example, if we follow through. We owe it to the flock to set an example, Sister Star.

"I know, I know. But it hurts my heart."

Judge Leverknight nodded soberly. "It does for all of us, Sister," she said. "None of us want this. None of us like this. As Sister Warner said, though, this will save souls. This will be remembered."

"I'll write up the verdict," offered Judge Warner. "Then we can send word to the Security Office. No need to reconvene."

The Security Office had two cells in the back of the building. Typically, both were empty. Currently, one was occupied. Elizabeth sat on the thin mattress on the metal bunk, quietly reading, when the door to the back room opened and multiple footsteps echoed in the corridor. Elizabeth looked up, fighting to push back the fear, and smiled happily when her friends stopped outside the small cell.

Michelle raised a hand, clutched a bar, and pressed her forehead against it. "Hi, sis," she said, softly.

Megan, always more exuberant, "Hi, Beth!"

"Hi, Beth. I'm sorry you're in here," said Christine, her normally impassive features threatening to burst with emotion.

"It's my own fault. I shouldn't have involved you, Michelle. I'm so sorry," said Elizabeth. "Don't be sad. I'll get through this. You'll see!"

"I was lucky," said Michelle. "I got off with a public paddling for not turning you in for dating unaccompanied." She rubbed her bottom ruefully with both hands. "That cute Security Officer, Wentworth – he can HIT!"

Megan giggled.

Elizabeth grinned for a moment, then looked troubled. "I don't know what my punishment is yet. Three days of Penance, followed by Grace, on the quad. That's all I know."

Christine frowned. "Three days in the stocks? What did they say was your Grace?"

Elizabeth shrugged. "They sent the preliminary verdict to Security earlier. The Detective let me read it. They didn't say what my Grace was. They said that...ummm..." She thought for a moment, then recited, carefully, from memory. "Upon conclusion, the final disposition of my soul shall be left to our Heavenly Father. Something like that." She shrugged.

Megan gasped. "Goodness! That sounds like you're gonna be whipped or caned!"

Elizabeth clutched the bars, leaning forward, pressing her forehead to the cool metal. "I don't know what it sounds like. It sounds awful. I don't understand...I didn't do wrong. I didn't break any laws."

Christine sighed, exasperated. "Elizabeth, in the eyes of the Church, of the Honor Court, you did more than just have an abortion. You engaged in promiscuous extramarital sex and murdered an infant. Like it or not, right or wrong in your eyes, that is their view. And, worse, you still don't own your sin. You don't accept the evil of what you did, choosing instead to wear it like some sort of badge of honor. That is the heart of what this is all about – accepting what you did and turning to Jesus for forgiveness. You rejected all of that and stood by the laws of man and Mammon, and not the Word of God. You refused forgiveness."

Elizabeth shook her head, angrily. "I'm sorry, but that's a load of nonsense. I know you believe it, but I don't!"

Michelle reached into the cell and wrapped her hand around Elizabeth's. "We'll be with you on the quad tomorrow, Elizabeth. I'm so sorry. They're calling out the entire dorm to watch your punishment."

Megan burst out, excitedly, "Everyone's talking about it, but no one knows what it is. Everyone's excited!"

"Megan!" exclaimed Christine, "This isn't a volleyball game!"

Megan hung her head. "I'm sorry, Beth. I...I'm just trying to look at the bright side, I guess."

Elizabeth smiled at her friend. "It's okay, Megan. I know people are talking. I don't blame them. I'm sure it's the story of the year."

"Of the century, more like!"

Elizabeth looked at Michelle. "I know it's to begin at 6am. I guess you all have to get up early for me!"

Michelle wrinkled her nose. "They even have the choir scheduled for it."

Elizabeth rolled her eyes and laughed. "The choir? Good God."

Christine touched Elizabeth's hand. "Listen to me. Please, listen. Just this once, Elizabeth. I brought a notebook and pen with me. Do you think...maybe...would you consider writing a letter to the Court? Asking forgiveness? Expressing remorse? Lots of remorse?"

Elizabeth frowned and shook her head. "No! I would rather be whipped than ask those creeps for anything!"

Christine tightened her grip on Elizabeth's hand, glanced up and down the corridor, and whispered, "Elizabeth, I don't think they're just gonna whip you. Please do this? If not for yourself, then for me? Please?"

Michelle nodded agreement. "It probably would be for the best. Maybe they'll reconsider whatever your punishment is, do something less severe? A paddling over the whip?"

Elizabeth frowned. She thought for a moment, then shook her head. "That would go against everything I believe in. I can't. I made my choice, and I believe it was the right one."

"You know they've sentenced students to a whole lot worse than whippings, Elizabeth," said Christine. "We've all heard the story about the one girl who was burned at the stake on the quad."

Megan shuddered. "Gosh, that musta sucked!"

Elizabeth rolled her eyes and smirked. "C'mon. That's nonsense. Just urban legends to scare the first years!"

"If you won't do the letter for yourself, would you for us? Your friends? It would make us feel better?" pleaded Christine.

Elizabeth shook her head, angrily. "I can't, Christine! You know that! You have your beliefs, and I have mine, and I can't do that! Would you ask forgiveness for your faith? Of course not. And I'm not gonna go begging for forgiveness to get out of a caning or a few days in the stupid stocks! What I did WAS not wrong!"

The door at the end of the corridor opened, and Officer Wentworth stuck his head in. "Ladies, time's up. Say good night, you'll see her tomorrow."

"Good night, Beth!" said Megan, "I'll see you tomorrow! Next week, let's go shopping!"

Elizabeth smiled at her ever-cheerful friend. "Sounds good, Meg. Love you."

Michelle whispered, "I'm sorry. I'm so sorry you're going through with this. I feel like it's all my fault."

Elizabeth shrugged and smiled. "We've been through worse when we were younger, sis. We'll get through this. I love you lots. We can get a coffee when this nonsense is over and I can sit straight again."

Michelle smiled. "Deal!"

Christine frowned. "I feel like I'm the only one who understands the gravity of the situation. I'll pray you for, Elizabeth. I love you like a sister, and I hope you actually accept Penance, accept Grace, and become my sister in Christ. I love you."

The sun was just breaking over the trees. Elizabeth squinted as the officers led her down the path of the campus quad.

As expected, she was roused early by Wentworth, at 4:30am, who handed her a bar of soap, a small bottle of shampoo, a towel, and the white garment penitents typically wore for punishments.

"It's a big morning for you, Elizabeth. Let's get you cleaned up and then go get this over with." He smiled at her.

"That sounds like a plan." She liked the campus cop. He was sweet. He meant well, she could tell.

After her shower – a blissfully hot one that steamed up the small bathroom wonderfully – she got dressed in the white garment. It was cut like a romper, covering her breasts and privates completely, preserving her modesty, but remaining wide open at the back, exposing her, shoulders and buttocks both. The garment ended nearly immediately where her thighs began, again, leaving her legs exposed.

Elizabeth did not have to wonder why. She knew it was for the whip.

Officer Wentworth walked at her right side. To her left was Officer Middleton. In front of them strode Detective Dennell, who looked miserable this morning. Elizabeth had teased him for his hang-dog expression before they left. "I'm the one who's going to get whipped, not you!" His dour expression had not changed, and he had not responded to her cheerfulness.

Behind them walked a minister, keeping pace, reading quietly from his Bible, too low to be heard by Elizabeth, who didn't really care anyway.

The sun was glaring brightly in her eyes. She squinted, trying to see ahead, and finally gave up, just lowering her eyes and staring at the beautiful red cobblestone of the path they walked.

In the distance, she could hear the choir singing. She tilted her head, making out the words, and smiled. She didn't consider herself a Christian, but she loved hymns, and the distant verses of "All is Well" echoed beautifully across the morning quad. Archaic sensibilities aside, St. Catherine of the Holy Cross had an amazing choir.

"Through the love of God our Savior, All will be well; Free and changeless is His favor; All, all is well.
Precious is the blood that healed us; Perfect is the grace that sealed us; Strong the hand stretched out to shield us; All must be well."

They passed the Administration building with its little pond, beautifully landscaped, and a gaggle of geese ushered their nearly-adult offspring away from the path, honking noisily at the three cops, minister, and penitent who passed. Another few days and they would be flying south. Elizabeth side-stepped goose droppings as they pressed forward.

"Though we pass through tribulation, All will be well; Ours is such a full salvation; All, all is well.
Happy still in God confiding, Fruitful, if in Christ abiding, Holy through the Spirit's guiding, All must be well."

The morning was brisk and chilly. Autumn was in the air. The leaves were already starting to change in the not-so-distant mountains. In another week, they would be changing here, too. She shivered in the thin white garment, but she relished the chill. She knew her flesh would, in all likelihood, feel the searing pain of the whip soon enough. The voices of the choir were louder, now.

"We expect a bright tomorrow; All will be well; Faith can sing through days of sorrow, All, all is well.

On our Father's love relying, Jesus every need supplying, Or in living, or in dying, All must be well."

The choir fell silent. Elizabeth looked up, squinting into the sun. She could barely make out a post, standing tall, in front of her, and a shorter beam on the ground at her feet. Wentworth and Middleton turned her around, and she faced her dormitory.

Her fellow students – her sisters – stood in rows, stoically, some 40 students. Several were crying. Elizabeth furrowed her brow. They weren't the ones being whipped, she thought.

The three Judges stood to the side. Judge Leverknight stepped forward. "Prefect, have you turned out all within your dorm as directed by the Honor Court?" she asked.

Christine stepped forward, her pleated black skirt ruffling. "Yes, Your Honor!"

Judge Leverknight nodded and she turned her head to face Elizabeth, who gazed impassively, expectantly, back. She unrolled a piece of paper, scanned it, then locked eyes with Elizabeth.

"Elizabeth Jones, you have been found guilty of murder in the first degree, of a three month old baby, whose name is known but to God."

Elizabeth glared. "I DID NOT!" she shouted. "I had an abortion!"

Judge Leverknight ignored her. "You have been sentenced to three days of Penance on the cross, one day for each month of the life your child was blessed with. You shall be nailed to the cross immediately. At 6 am, three days from now, your knees will be broken. Shortly after, you shall receive your final Grace from God above, before Whom you shall stand in judgement."

Elizabeth blinked. "Wait, what?" The crowd of girls murmured, horrified. "WHAT DID YOU SAY? WHAT IS THIS? WHAT ARE YOU SAYING?" screamed Elizabeth.

Judge Leverknight tucked the paper away. "Officer Wentworth, Officer Middleton, Detective Dennell, place her on the cross, please."

The judge started to turn away, then paused. "Miss Jones, I beg of you, to pray over the next three days. To pray hard, and to search for the salvation that is still yours, if you want it."

Elizabeth stared, stunned, unmoving, even as Officer Wentworth took her right arm and Middleton seized her left. "What is this?" she screamed, "You can't do this!"

Someone tripped her as the two security officers hauled her backwards and lowered her to the ground. Both pinned her to the beam, quickly binding her wrists to the cross. Elizabeth stared in stunned horror as she was spread out, her legs flailing. A moment later they were pinned and her ankles bound.

"Please don't," she whispered, "I'm sorry, I'm sorry, I didn't know what I was doing!"

The detective knelt by her left arm. "I'm sorry, Miss Jones," he murmured. He felt her wrist, probing at it with his thumb.

"What are you doing? Stop! Please, stop!" wailed Elizabeth, "I'm sorry! That's what you wanted to hear, isn't it?"

Detective Dennell pressed a nail, impossibly long, impossibly thick, to her bound wrist. Elizabeth stopped screaming, watching as the hammer raised high, higher, into the morning sun, blinding her, and then, as the hammer fell, as the shrieks of agony echoed across the campus, the choir started again.

"What a friend we have in Jesus! All our sins and griefs to bear! What a privilege to carry Everything to God in prayer!"

"No! NOOO! THIS IS NOT HAPPENING!" The hammer clanged, steel on steel, once, twice, three times, until the wide head pressed against her wrist. She was thrashing, trying to kick, but the ropes held her securely, and both Middleton and Wentworth were pressing her shoulders to the wood.

"Oh, what peace we often forfeit! Oh, what needless pain we bear! All because we do not carry Everything to God in prayer!"

The detective was at her right arm, probing her wrist. He was trying to ignore her, focused on his duty.

"IT HURTS, PLEASE, NO MORE NAILS, NO MORE, PLEASE!"

Dennell grunted, "Okay, hold her steady." Wentworth and Middleton pressed her down. Again, the hammer rose and fell, and renewed screams of agony echoed against the beautiful stone buildings that graced the quad.

"OH GOD OH GOD I'M SORRY IT HURTS PLEASE PLEEEAAASE NO MORE!"

They dragged the beam backward, dragging Elizabeth over the ground, until she could see the upright towering over her head. She thrashed against her beam, waves of agony rolling down her arms, her hands frozen in a rictus of never-ending pain.

"Have we trials and temptations? Is there trouble anywhere?
We should never be discouraged, Take it to the Lord in prayer!"

"Lift with your legs, not your backs." Dennell selected two more nails as the two officers, together, hefted the crossbeam upward. Elizabeth frantically struggled for any position less painful as they lifted, rotating the beam forward, and she gasped in pain, gritting her teeth, first getting her knees under her, then her bound feet.

"On a count of three, now. One...two...three!"

And they lifted her, higher, pushing the beam up over the top of the upright until it slid down and jolted in place on the joint above. One of them secured it as Elizabeth dangled by her bound and nailed wrists, her diaphragm heaving, mouth agape, gasping for breath. Wentworth grabbed her bound feet and pushed them up on a narrowly sloped slab of wood fixed to the upright. Her knees straightened as she shot upright, shrieking.

"Can we find a friend so faithful? Who will all our sorrows share? Jesus knows our every weakness! Take it to the Lord in prayer"

"I got her legs, hurry up..."

Inspector Dennell knelt in front of her. "Press them flat against the upright...that's it..."

The nail exploded through the top of her left foot and she sagged down, sobbing. Her throat was on fire already from screaming, and she shook as the spasms wracked her arms.

"OH GOD DADDY DADDY MOMMY I'M SORRY I'M SO SORRY PLEASE HELP ME!"

"Are we weak and heavy-laden, Cumbered with a load of care? Precious Savior, still our refuge, Take it to the Lord in prayer!"

She lifted her head, shaking it to the left and right, willing the nightmare to be over. She saw Michelle, vomiting, on her knees, and Megan standing, horrified, staring at her, transfixed. A moment later, Michelle was rushing away, sobbing hysterically. No one moved to stop her. Christine stood next to them, gazing at her with sorrow.

The final nail was pounded in place. A short barking shriek, and she sagged against the cross, her back scraping down the rough wood.

"Do thy friends despise, forsake thee? Take it to the Lord in prayer!

In His arms He'll take and shield thee! Thou wilt find a solace there."

The choir died down again.

"Good job, brothers," said Judge Leverknight. The three security officers stepped back, gazing up at their work.

For just a moment, the campus was blissfully silent, only to be shattered when Elizabeth found the strength to begin screaming again.

"OH GOD OH GOD OH JESUS GODDD I'M SORRRRRYYYYYY IT HURRRTSSS!!!!!"

As the shrieks echoed across the campus, the choir again picked up, their heavenly voices blending with the agony of the damned.

"Amazing grace how sweet the sound, That saved a wretch like me!
I once was lost, but now I'm found! Was blind but now I see!
'Twas grace that taught my heart to fear, and grace my fears relieved!
How precious did that grace appear, the hour I first believed!
Through many dangers, toils, and snares, I have already come,
This grace that brought me safe thus far, and grace will lead me
home!
When we've been here ten thousand years, bright, shining as the sun,
We've no less days to sing God's praise, than when we first begun!
Amazing grace how sweet the sound, that saved a wretch like me!
I once was lost, but now I'm found, was blind but now I see!"

Finit

www.ingramcontent.com/pod-product-compliance
Lightning Source LLC
Chambersburg PA
CBHW051456050726

47593CB00005B/2098